Samuel Langhorne Clemens (November 30, 1835 – April 21, 1910), known by his pen name Mark Twain, was an American writer, humorist, entrepreneur, publisher, and lecturer. He was lauded as the "greatest humorist this country has produced", and William Faulkner called him "the father of American literature". His novels include The Adventures of Tom Sawyer (1876) and its sequel, the Adventures of Huckleberry Finn (1884), the latter often called "The Great American Novel".

Twain was raised in Hannibal, Missouri, which later provided the setting for Tom Sawyer and Huckleberry Finn. He served an apprenticeship with a printer and then worked as a typesetter, contributing articles to the newspaper of his older brother Orion Clemens. He later became a riverboat pilot on the Mississippi River before heading west to join Orion in Nevada. (Source: Wikipedia)

Literary works:
The Gilded Age: A Tale of Today (1873)
The Prince and the Pauper (1881)
A Connecticut Yankee in
King Arthur's Court (1889)
The American Claimant (1892)
Pudd'nhead Wilson (1894)
Personal Recollections of Joan of Arc (1896)
A Horse's Tale (1907)
The Mysterious Stranger (1916, posthumous)
The Adventures of Tom Sawyer (1876)
Adventures of Huckleberry Finn (1884)
Tom Sawyer Abroad (1894)
Tom Sawyer, Detective (1896)
"Eve's Diary" (1906)

IS SHAKESPEARE DEAD?

MARK TWAIN

PRINCE CLASSICS

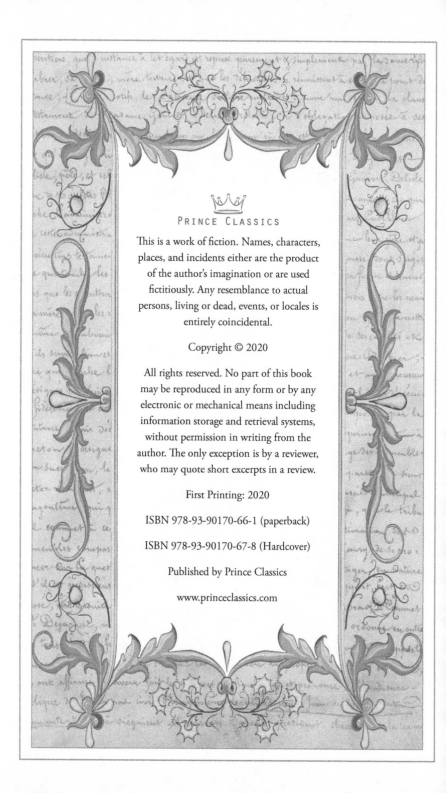

PRINCE CLASSICS

First Printing: 2020

ISBN 978-93-90170-66-1 (paperback)

ISBN 978-93-90170-67-8 (Hardcover)

Published by Prince Classics

www.princeclassics.com

Contents

IS SHAKESPEARE DEAD?

CHAPTER I

Scattered here and there through the stacks of unpublished manuscript which constitute this formidable Autobiography and Diary of mine, certain chapters will in some distant future be found which deal with "Claimants"— claimants historically notorious: Satan, Claimant; the Golden Calf, Claimant; the Veiled Prophet of Khorassan, Claimant; Louis XVII., Claimant; William Shakespeare, Claimant; Arthur Orton, Claimant; Mary Baker G. Eddy, Claimant—and the rest of them. Eminent Claimants, successful Claimants, defeated Claimants, royal Claimants, pleb Claimants, showy Claimants, shabby Claimants, revered Claimants, despised Claimants, twinkle starlike here and there and yonder through the mists of history and legend and tradition—and oh, all the darling tribe are clothed in mystery and romance, and we read about them with deep interest and discuss them with loving sympathy or with rancorous resentment, according to which side we hitch ourselves to. It has always been so with the human race. There was never a Claimant that couldn't get a hearing, nor one that couldn't accumulate a rapturous following, no matter how flimsy and apparently unauthentic his claim might be. Arthur Orton's claim that he was the lost Tichborne baronet come to life again was as flimsy as Mrs. Eddy's that she wrote *Science and Health* from the direct dictation of the Deity; yet in England near forty years ago Orton had a huge army of devotees and incorrigible adherents, many of whom remained stubbornly unconvinced after their fat god had been proven an impostor and jailed as a perjurer, and to-day Mrs. Eddy's following is not only immense, but is daily augmenting in numbers and enthusiasm. Orton had many fine and educated minds among his adherents, Mrs. Eddy has had the like among hers from the beginning. Her church is as well equipped in those particulars as is any other church. Claimants can always count upon a following, it doesn't matter who they are, nor what they claim, nor whether they come with documents or without. It was always so. Down out of the long-vanished past, across the abyss of the ages, if you listen you can still hear the believing multitudes shouting for Perkin Warbeck and Lambert Simnel.

A friend has sent me a new book, from England—*The Shakespeare Problem Restated*—well restated and closely reasoned; and my fifty years' interest in that matter—asleep for the last three years—is excited once more. It is an interest which was born of Delia Bacon's book—away back in that ancient day—1857, or maybe 1856. About a year later my pilot-master, Bixby, transferred me from his own steamboat to the *Pennsylvania*, and placed me under the orders and instructions of George Ealer—dead now, these many, many years. I steered for him a good many months—as was the humble duty of the pilot-apprentice: stood a daylight watch and spun the wheel under the severe superintendence and correction of the master. He was a prime chess player and an idolater of Shakespeare. He would play chess with anybody; even with me, and it cost his official dignity something to do that. Also—quite uninvited—he would read Shakespeare to me; not just casually, but by the hour, when it was his watch, and I was steering. He read well, but not profitably for me, because he constantly injected commands into the text. That broke it all up, mixed it all up, tangled it all up—to that degree, in fact, that if we were in a risky and difficult piece of river an ignorant person couldn't have told, sometimes, which observations were Shakespeare's and which were Ealer's. For instance:

What man dare, *I* dare!

Approach thou *what* are you laying in the leads for? what a hell of an idea! like the rugged ease her off a little, ease her off! rugged Russian bear, the armed rhinoceros or the *there* she goes! meet her, meet her! didn't you *know* she'd smell the reef if you crowded it like that? Hyrcan tiger; take any shape but that and my firm nerves she'll be in the *woods* the first you know! stop the starboard! come ahead strong on the larboard! back the starboard! . . . *Now* then, you're all right; come ahead on the starboard; straighten up and go 'long, never tremble: or be alive again, and dare me to the desert damnation can't you keep away from that greasy water? pull her down! snatch her! snatch her baldheaded! with thy sword; if trembling I inhabit then, lay in the leads!—no, only the starboard one, leave the other alone, protest me the baby of a girl. Hence horrible shadow! eight bells—that watchman's asleep again, I reckon, go down and call Brown yourself, unreal mockery, hence!

He certainly was a good reader, and splendidly thrilling and stormy and tragic, but it was a damage to me, because I have never since been able to read Shakespeare in a calm and sane way. I cannot rid it of his explosive interlardings, they break in everywhere with their irrelevant "What in hell are you up to *now*! pull her down! more! *more*!—there now, steady as you go," and the other disorganizing interruptions that were always leaping from his mouth. When I read Shakespeare now, I can hear them as plainly as I did in that long-departed time—fifty-one years ago. I never regarded Ealer's readings as educational. Indeed they were a detriment to me.

His contributions to the text seldom improved it, but barring that detail he was a good reader, I can say that much for him. He did not use the book, and did not need to; he knew his Shakespeare as well as Euclid ever knew his multiplication table.

Did he have something to say—this Shakespeare-adoring Mississippi pilot—anent Delia Bacon's book? Yes. And he said it; said it all the time, for months—in the morning watch, the middle watch, the dog watch; and probably kept it going in his sleep. He bought the literature of the dispute as fast as it appeared, and we discussed it all through thirteen hundred miles of river four times traversed in every thirty-five days—the time required by that swift boat to achieve two round trips. We discussed, and discussed, and discussed, and disputed and disputed and disputed; at any rate he did, and I got in a word now and then when he slipped a cog and there was a vacancy. He did his arguing with heat, with energy, with violence; and I did mine with the reserve and moderation of a subordinate who does not like to be flung out of a pilot-house that is perched forty feet above the water. He was fiercely loyal to Shakespeare and cordially scornful of Bacon and of all the pretensions of the Baconians. So was I—at first. And at first he was glad that that was my attitude. There were even indications that he admired it; indications

11

dimmed, it is true, by the distance that lay between the lofty boss-pilotical altitude and my lowly one, yet perceptible to me; perceptible, and translatable into a compliment—compliment coming down from above the snow-line and not well thawed in the transit, and not likely to set anything afire, not even a cub-pilot's self-conceit; still a detectable compliment, and precious.

Naturally it flattered me into being more loyal to Shakespeare—if possible—than I was before, and more prejudiced against Bacon—if possible than I was before. And so we discussed and discussed, both on the same side, and were happy. For a while. Only for a while. Only for a very little while, a very, very, very little while. Then the atmosphere began to change; began to cool off.

A brighter person would have seen what the trouble was, earlier than I did, perhaps, but I saw it early enough for all practical purposes. You see, he was of an argumentative disposition. Therefore it took him but a little time to get tired of arguing with a person who agreed with everything he said and consequently never furnished him a provocative to flare up and show what he could do when it came to clear, cold, hard, rose-cut, hundred-faceted, diamond-flashing reasoning. That was his name for it. It has been applied since, with complacency, as many as several times, in the Bacon-Shakespeare scuffle. On the Shakespeare side.

Then the thing happened which has happened to more persons than to me when principle and personal interest found themselves in opposition to each other and a choice had to be made: I let principle go, and went over to the other side. Not the entire way, but far enough to answer the requirements of the case. That is to say, I took this attitude, to wit: I only *believed* Bacon wrote Shakespeare, whereas I *knew* Shakespeare didn't. Ealer was satisfied with that, and the war broke loose. Study, practice, experience in handling my end of the matter presently enabled me to take my new position almost seriously; a little bit later, utterly seriously; a little later still, lovingly, gratefully, devotedly; finally: fiercely, rabidly, uncompromisingly. After that, I was welded to my faith, I was theoretically ready to die for it, and I looked down with compassion not unmixed with scorn, upon everybody else's faith that didn't tally with mine. That faith, imposed upon me by self-interest in that ancient day, remains my faith to-day, and in it I find comfort, solace, peace, and never-failing joy. You see how curiously theological it is. The "rice Christian" of the Orient goes through the very same steps, when he is after rice and the missionary is after *him*; he goes for rice, and remains to worship.

Ealer did a lot of our "reasoning"—not to say substantially all of it. The slaves of his cult have a passion for calling it by that large name. We others do not call our inductions and deductions and reductions by any name at all. They show for themselves, what they are, and we can with tranquil confidence leave the world to ennoble them with a title of its own choosing.

Now and then when Ealer had to stop to cough, I pulled my induction-talents together and hove the controversial lead myself: always getting eight feet, eight-and-a-half, often nine, sometimes even quarter-less-twain—as *I* believed; but always "no bottom," as *he* said.

I got the best of him only once. I prepared myself. I wrote out a passage from Shakespeare—it may have been the very one I quoted a while ago, I don't remember—and riddled it with his wild steamboatful interlardings. When an unrisky opportunity offered, one lovely summer day, when we had sounded and buoyed a tangled patch of crossings known as Hell's Half Acre, and were aboard again and he had sneaked the Pennsylvania triumphantly through it without once scraping sand, and the *A. T. Lacey* had followed in our wake and got stuck, and he was feeling good, I showed it to him. It amused him. I asked him to fire it off: read it; read it, I diplomatically added, as only he could read dramatic poetry. The compliment touched him where he lived. He did read it; read it with surpassing fire and spirit; read it as it will never be read again; for *he* knew how to put the right music into those thunderous interlardings and make them seem a part of the text, make them sound as if they were bursting from Shakespeare's own soul, each one of them a golden inspiration and not to be left out without damage to the massed and magnificent whole.

I waited a week, to let the incident fade; waited longer; waited until he brought up for reasonings and vituperation my pet position, my pet argument, the one which I was fondest of, the one which I prized far above

13

all others in my ammunition-wagon, to wit: that Shakespeare couldn't have written Shakespeare's works, for the reason that the man who wrote them was limitlessly familiar with the laws, and the law-courts, and law-proceedings, and lawyer-talk, and lawyer-ways—and if Shakespeare was possessed of the infinitely-divided star-dust that constituted this vast wealth, how did he get it, and *where*, and *when*?

"From books."

From books! That was always the idea. I answered as my readings of the champions of my side of the great controversy had taught me to answer: that a man can't handle glibly and easily and comfortably and successfully the *argot* of a trade at which he has not personally served. He will make mistakes; he will not, and cannot, get the trade-phrasings precisely and exactly right; and the moment he departs, by even a shade, from a common trade-form, the reader who has served that trade will know the writer *hasn't*. Ealer would not be convinced; he said a man could learn how to correctly handle the subtleties and mysteries and free-masonries of any trade by careful reading and studying. But when I got him to read again the passage from Shakespeare with the interlardings, he perceived, himself, that books couldn't teach a student a bewildering multitude of pilot-phrases so thoroughly and perfectly that he could talk them off in book and play or conversation and make no mistake that a pilot would not immediately discover. It was a triumph for me. He was silent awhile, and I knew what was happening: he was losing his temper. And I knew he would presently close the session with the same old argument that was always his stay and his support in time of need; the same old argument, the one I couldn't answer—because I dasn't: the argument that I was an ass, and better shut up. He delivered it, and I obeyed.

Oh, dear, how long ago it was—how pathetically long ago! And here am I, old, forsaken, forlorn and alone, arranging to get that argument out of somebody again.

When a man has a passion for Shakespeare, it goes without saying that he keeps company with other standard authors. Ealer always had several high-class books in the pilot-house, and he read the same ones over and over again, and did not care to change to newer and fresher ones. He played well on the flute, and greatly enjoyed hearing himself play. So did I. He had a notion that a flute would keep its health better if you took it apart when it was not standing a watch; and so, when it was not on duty it took its rest, disjointed, on the compass-shelf under the breast-board. When the *Pennsylvania* blew up and became a drifting rack-heap freighted with wounded and dying poor souls (my young brother Henry among them), pilot Brown had the watch below, and was probably asleep and never knew what killed him; but Ealer escaped unhurt. He and his pilot-house were shot up into the air; then they fell, and Ealer sank through the ragged cavern where the hurricane deck and the boiler deck had been, and landed in a nest of ruins on the main deck, on top of one of the unexploded boilers, where he lay prone in a fog of scalding and deadly steam. But not for long. He did not lose his head: long familiarity with danger had taught him to keep it, in any and all emergencies. He held his coat-lappels to his nose with one hand, to keep out the steam, and scrabbled around with the other till he found the joints of his flute, then he is took measures to save himself alive, and was successful. I was not on board. I had been put ashore in New Orleans by Captain Klinefelter. The reason—however, I have told all about it in the book called *Old Times on the Mississippi*, and it isn't important anyway, it is so long ago.

CHAPTER II

When I was a Sunday-school scholar something more than sixty years ago, I became interested in Satan, and wanted to find out all I could about him. I began to ask questions, but my class-teacher, Mr. Barclay the stone-mason, was reluctant about answering them, it seemed to me. I was anxious to be praised for turning my thoughts to serious subjects when there wasn't another boy in the village who could be hired to do such a thing. I was greatly interested in the incident of Eve and the serpent, and thought Eve's calmness was perfectly noble. I asked Mr. Barclay if he had ever heard of another woman who, being approached by a serpent, would not excuse herself and break for the nearest timber. He did not answer my question, but rebuked me for inquiring into matters above my age and comprehension. I will say for Mr. Barclay that he was willing to tell me the facts of Satan's history, but he stopped there: he wouldn't allow any discussion of them.

In the course of time we exhausted the facts. There were only five or six of them, you could set them all down on a visiting-card. I was disappointed. I had been meditating a biography, and was grieved to find that there were no materials. I said as much, with the tears running down. Mr. Barclay's sympathy and compassion were aroused, for he was a most kind and gentle-spirited man, and he patted me on the head and cheered me up by saying there was a whole vast ocean of materials! I can still feel the happy thrill which these blessed words shot through me.

Then he began to bail out that ocean's riches for my encouragement and joy. Like this: it was "conjectured"—though not established—that Satan was originally an angel in heaven; that he fell; that he rebelled, and brought on a war; that he was defeated, and banished to perdition. Also, "we have reason to believe" that later he did so-and-so; that "we are warranted in supposing" that at a subsequent time he travelled extensively, seeking whom he might devour; that a couple of centuries afterward, "as tradition instructs us," he took up the cruel trade of tempting people to their ruin, with vast and fearful results; that by-and-by, "as the probabilities seem to indicate," he may have done certain things, he might have done certain other things, he must have done still other things.

And so on and so on. We set down the five known facts by themselves, on a piece of paper, and numbered it "page 1"; then on fifteen hundred other pieces of paper we set down the "conjectures," and "suppositions," and "maybes," and "perhapses," and "doubtlesses," and "rumors," and "guesses," and "probabilities," and "likelihoods," and "we are permitted to thinks," and "we are warranted in believings," and "might have beens," and "could have beens," and "must have beens," and "unquestionablys," and "without a shadow of doubts"—and behold!

Materials? Why, we had enough to build a biography of Shakespeare!

Yet he made me put away my pen; he would not let me write the history of Satan. Why? Because, as he said, he had suspicions; suspicions that my attitude in this matter was not reverent; and that a person must be reverent when writing about the sacred characters. He said any one who spoke flippantly of Satan would be frowned upon by the religious world and also be brought to account.

I assured him, in earnest and sincere words, that he had wholly misconceived my attitude; that I had the highest respect for Satan, and that my reverence for him equalled, and possibly even exceeded, that of any member of any church. I said it wounded me deeply to perceive by his words that he thought I would make fun of Satan, and deride him, laugh at him, scoff at him: whereas in truth I had never thought of such a thing, but had only a warm desire to make fun of those others and laugh at *them.* "What others?" "Why, the Supposers, the Perhapsers, the Might-Have-Beeners, the Could-Have-Beeners, the Must-Have-Beeners, the Without-a-Shadow-of-Doubters, the We-are-Warranted-in-Believingers, and all that funny crop of solemn architects who have taken a good solid foundation of five indisputable and unimportant facts and built upon it a Conjectural Satan thirty miles high."

17

What did Mr. Barclay do then? Was he disarmed? Was he silenced? No. He was shocked. He was so shocked that he visibly shuddered. He said the Satanic Traditioners and Perhapsers and Conjecturers were *themselves* sacred! As sacred as their work. So sacred that whoso ventured to mock them or make fun of their work, could not afterward enter any respectable house, even by the back door.

How true were his words, and how wise! How fortunate it would have been for me if I had heeded them. But I was young, I was but seven years of age, and vain, foolish, and anxious to attract attention. I wrote the biography, and have never been in a respectable house since.

CHAPTER III

How curious and interesting is the parallel—as far as poverty of biographical details is concerned—between Satan and Shakespeare. It is wonderful, it is unique, it stands quite alone, there is nothing resembling it in history, nothing resembling it in romance, nothing approaching it even in tradition. How sublime is their position, and how over-topping, how sky-reaching, how supreme—the two Great Unknowns, the two Illustrious Conjecturabilities! They are the best-known unknown persons that have ever drawn breath upon the planet.

For the instruction of the ignorant I will make a list, now, of those details of Shakespeare's history which are *facts*—verified facts, established facts, undisputed facts.

FACTS

He was born on the 23d of April, 1564.

Of good farmer-class parents who could not read, could not write, could not sign their names.

At Stratford, a small back settlement which in that day was shabby and unclean, and densely illiterate. Of the nineteen important men charged with the government of the town, thirteen had to "make their mark" in attesting important documents, because they could not write their names.

Of the first eighteen years of his life *nothing* is known. They are a blank.

On the 27th of November (1582) William Shakespeare took out a license to marry Anne Whateley.

Next day William Shakespeare took out a license to marry Anne Hathaway. She was eight years his senior.

William Shakespeare married Anne Hathaway. In a hurry. By grace of a reluctantly-granted dispensation there was but one publication of the banns.

Within six months the first child was born.

About two (blank) years followed, during which period *nothing at all happened to Shakespeare*, so far as anybody knows.

Then came twins—1585. February.

Two blank years follow.

Then—1587—he makes a ten-year visit to London, leaving the family behind.

Five blank years follow. During this period *nothing happened to him*, as far as anybody actually knows.

Then—1592—there is mention of him as an actor.

Next year—1593—his name appears in the official list of players.

Next year—1594—he played before the queen. A detail of no consequence: other obscurities did it every year of the forty-five of her reign. And remained obscure.

Three pretty full years follow. Full of play-acting. Then

In 1597 he bought New Place, Stratford.

Thirteen or fourteen busy years follow; years in which he accumulated money, and also reputation as actor and manager.

Meantime his name, liberally and variously spelt, had become associated with a number of great plays and poems, as (ostensibly) author of the same.

Some of these, in these years and later, were pirated, but he made no protest. Then—1610-11—he returned to Stratford and settled down for good and all, and busied himself in lending money, trading in tithes, trading in land and houses; shirking a debt of forty-one shillings, borrowed by his wife during his long desertion of his family; suing debtors for shillings and coppers; being sued himself for shillings and coppers; and acting as confederate to a neighbor who tried to rob the town of its rights in a certain common, and did not succeed.

He lived five or six years—till 1616—in the joy of these elevated pursuits. Then he made a will, and signed each of its three pages with his name.

A thoroughgoing business man's will. It named in minute detail every item of property he owned in the world—houses, lands, sword, silver-gilt bowl, and so on—all the way down to his "second-best bed" and its furniture.

It carefully and calculatingly distributed his riches among the members of his family, overlooking no individual of it. Not even his wife: the wife he had been enabled to marry in a hurry by urgent grace of a special dispensation before he was nineteen; the wife whom he had left husbandless so many years; the wife who had had to borrow forty-one shillings in her need, and which the lender was never able to collect of the prosperous husband, but died at last with the money still lacking. No, even this wife was remembered in Shakespeare's will.

He left her that "second-best bed."

And *not another thing*; not even a penny to bless her lucky widowhood with.

It was eminently and conspicuously a business man's will, not a poet's.

It mentioned *not a single book*.

Books were much more precious than swords and silver-gilt bowls and second-best beds in those days, and when a departing person owned one he gave it a high place in his will.

The will mentioned *not a play, not a poem, not an unfinished literary work, not a scrap of manuscript of any kind.*

Many poets have died poor, but this is the only one in history that has died *this* poor; the others all left literary remains behind. Also a book. Maybe two.

If Shakespeare had owned a dog—but we need not go into that: we know he would have mentioned it in his will. If a good dog, Susanna would have got it; if an inferior one his wife would have got a dower interest in it. I wish he had had a dog, just so we could see how painstakingly he would have divided that dog among the family, in his careful business way.

He signed the will in three places.

In earlier years he signed two other official documents.

These five signatures still exist.

There are *no other specimens of his penmanship in existence.* Not a line.

Was he prejudiced against the art? His granddaughter, whom he loved, was eight years old when he died, yet she had had no teaching, he left no provision for her education although he was rich, and in her mature womanhood she couldn't write and couldn't tell her husband's manuscript from anybody else's—she thought it was Shakespeare's.

When Shakespeare died in Stratford *it was not an event.* It made no more stir in England than the death of any other forgotten theatre-actor would have made. Nobody came down from London; there were no lamenting poems, no eulogies, no national tears—there was merely silence, and nothing more. A striking contrast with what happened when Ben Jonson, and Francis Bacon, and Spenser, and Raleigh and the other distinguished literary folk of Shakespeare's time passed from life! No praiseful voice was lifted for the lost Bard of Avon; even Ben Jonson waited seven years before he lifted his.

So far as anybody actually knows and can prove, Shakespeare of Stratford-on-Avon never wrote a play in his life.

So far as anybody knows and can prove, he never wrote a letter to anybody in his life.

So far as any one knows, he received only one letter during his life.

So far as any one *knows and can prove,* Shakespeare of Stratford wrote only one poem during his life. This one is authentic. He did write that one—a fact which stands undisputed; he wrote the whole of it; he wrote the whole of it out of his own head. He commanded that this work of art be engraved upon his tomb, and he was obeyed. There it abides to this day. This is it:

22

Good friend for Iesus sake forbeare

To digg the dust encloased heare:

Blest be ye man yt spares thes stones

And curst be he yt moves my bones.

In the list as above set down, will be found *every positively known* fact of Shakespeare's life, lean and meagre as the invoice is. Beyond these details we know *not a thing* about him. All the rest of his vast history, as furnished by the biographers, is built up, course upon course, of guesses, inferences, theories, conjectures—an Eiffel Tower of artificialities rising sky-high from a very flat and very thin foundation of inconsequential facts.

CHAPTER IV—CONJECTURES

The historians "suppose" that Shakespeare attended the Free School in Stratford from the time he was seven years old till he was thirteen. There is no *evidence* in existence that he ever went to school at all.

The historians "infer" that he got his Latin in that school—the school which they "suppose" he attended.

They "suppose" his father's declining fortunes made it necessary for him to leave the school they supposed he attended, and get to work and help support his parents and their ten children. But there is no evidence that he ever entered or retired from the school they suppose he attended.

They "suppose" he assisted his father in the butchering business; and that, being only a boy, he didn't have to do full-grown butchering, but only slaughtered calves. Also, that whenever he killed a calf he made a high-flown speech over it. This supposition rests upon the testimony of a man who wasn't there at the time; a man who got it from a man who could have been there, but did not say whether he was or not; and neither of them thought to mention it for decades, and decades, and decades, and two more decades after Shakespeare's death (until old age and mental decay had refreshed and vivified their memories). They hadn't two facts in stock about the long-dead distinguished citizen, but only just the one: he slaughtered calves and broke into oratory while he was at it. Curious. They had only one fact, yet the distinguished citizen had spent twenty-six years in that little town—just half his lifetime. However, rightly viewed, it was the most important fact, indeed almost the only important fact, of Shakespeare's life in Stratford. Rightly viewed. For experience is an author's most valuable asset; experience is the thing that puts the muscle and the breath and the warm blood into the book he writes. Rightly viewed, calf-butchering accounts for *Titus Andronicus*, the only play—ain't it?—that the Stratford Shakespeare ever wrote; and yet it is the only one everybody tries to chouse him out of, the Baconians included.

The historians find themselves "justified in believing" that the young Shakespeare poached upon Sir Thomas Lucy's deer preserves and got haled before that magistrate for it. But there is no shred of respectworthy evidence that anything of the kind happened.

The historians, having argued the thing that *might* have happened into the thing that *did* happen, found no trouble in turning Sir Thomas Lucy into Mr. Justice Shallow. They have long ago convinced the world—on surmise and without trustworthy evidence—that Shallow *is* Sir Thomas.

The next addition to the young Shakespeare's Stratford history comes easy. The historian builds it out of the surmised deer-stealing, and the surmised trial before the magistrate, and the surmised vengeance-prompted satire upon the magistrate in the play: result, the young Shakespeare was a wild, wild, wild, oh *such* a wild young scamp, and that gratuitous slander is established for all time! It is the very way Professor Osborn and I built the colossal skeleton brontosaur that stands fifty-seven feet long and sixteen feet high in the Natural History Museum, the awe and admiration of all the world, the stateliest skeleton that exists on the planet. We had nine bones, and we built the rest of him out of plaster of paris. We ran short of plaster of paris, or we'd have built a brontosaur that could sit down beside the Stratford Shakespeare and none but an expert could tell which was biggest or contained the most plaster.

Shakespeare pronounced *Venus and Adonis* "the first heir of his invention," apparently implying that it was his first effort at literary composition. He should not have said it. It has been an embarrassment to his historians these many, many years. They have to make him write that graceful and polished and flawless and beautiful poem before he escaped from Stratford and his family—1586 or '87—age, twenty-two, or along there; because within the next five years he wrote five great plays, and could not have found time to write another line.

It is sorely embarrassing. If he began to slaughter calves, and poach deer, and rollick around, and learn English, at the earliest likely moment—say at thirteen, when he was supposably wrenched from that school where he was supposably storing up Latin for future literary use—he had his youthful hands full, and much more than full. He must have had to put aside his Warwickshire dialect, which wouldn't be understood in London, and study English very hard. Very hard indeed; incredibly hard, almost, if the result of that labor was to be the smooth and rounded and flexible and letter-perfect English of the *Venus and Adonis* in the space of ten years; and at the same time learn great and fine and unsurpassable literary form.

However, it is "conjectured" that he accomplished all this and more, much more: learned law and its intricacies; and the complex procedure of the law courts; and all about soldiering, and sailoring, and the manners and customs and ways of royal courts and aristocratic society; and likewise accumulated in his one head every kind of knowledge the learned then possessed, and every kind of humble knowledge possessed by the lowly and the ignorant; and added thereto a wider and more intimate knowledge of the world's great literatures, ancient and modern, than was possessed by any other man of his time—for he was going to make brilliant and easy and admiration-compelling use of these splendid treasures the moment he got to London. And according to the surmisers, that is what he did. Yes, although there was no one in Stratford able to teach him these things, and no library in the little village to dig them out of. His father could not read, and even the surmisers surmise that he did not keep a library.

It is surmised by the biographers that the young Shakespeare got his vast knowledge of the law and his familiar and accurate acquaintance with the manners and customs and shop-talk of lawyers through being for a time the *clerk of a Stratford court*; just as a bright lad like me, reared in a village on the banks of the Mississippi, might become perfect in knowledge of the Behring Strait whale-fishery and the shop-talk of the veteran exercisers of that adventure-bristling trade through catching catfish with a "trot-line" Sundays. But the surmise is damaged by the fact that there is no evidence—and not even tradition—that the young Shakespeare was ever clerk of a law court.

It is further surmised that the young Shakespeare accumulated his law-treasures in the first years of his sojourn in London, through "amusing himself" by learning book-law in his garret and by picking up lawyer-talk and the rest of it through loitering about the law-courts and listening. But it is only surmise; there is no *evidence* that he ever did either of those things. They are merely a couple of chunks of plaster of paris.

There is a legend that he got his bread and butter by holding horses in front of the London theatres, mornings and afternoons. Maybe he did. If he did, it seriously shortened his law-study hours and his recreation-time in the courts. In those very days he was writing great plays, and needed all the time he could get. The horse-holding legend ought to be strangled; it too formidably increases the historian's difficulty in accounting for the young Shakespeare's erudition—an erudition which he was acquiring, hunk by hunk and chunk by chunk every day in those strenuous times, and emptying each day's catch into next day's imperishable drama.

He had to acquire a knowledge of war at the same time; and a knowledge of soldier-people and sailor-people and their ways and talk; also a knowledge of some foreign lands and their languages: for he was daily emptying fluent streams of these various knowledges, too, into his dramas. How did he acquire these rich assets?

In the usual way: by surmise. It is *surmised* that he travelled in Italy and Germany and around, and qualified himself to put their scenic and social aspects upon paper; that he perfected himself in French, Italian and Spanish on the road; that he went in Leicester's expedition to the Low Countries, as soldier or sutler or something, for several months or years—or whatever length of time a surmiser needs in his business—and thus became familiar with soldiership and soldier-ways and soldier-talk, and generalship and general-ways and general-talk, and seamanship and sailor-ways and sailor-talk.

Maybe he did all these things, but I would like to know who held the horses in the meantime; and who studied the books in the garret; and who frollicked in the law-courts for recreation. Also, who did the call-boying and the play-acting.

For he became a call-boy; and as early as '93 he became a "vagabond"— the law's ungentle term for an unlisted actor; and in '94 a "regular" and properly and officially listed member of that (in those days) lightly-valued and not much respected profession.

Right soon thereafter he became a stockholder in two theatres, and manager of them. Thenceforward he was a busy and flourishing business man, and was raking in money with both hands for twenty years. Then in a noble frenzy of poetic inspiration he wrote his one poem—his only poem, his darling—and laid him down and died:

> Good friend for Iesus sake forbeare
>
> To digg the dust encloased heare:
>
> Blest be ye man yt spares thes stones
>
> And curst be he yt moves my bones.

He was probably dead when he wrote it. Still, this is only conjecture. We have only circumstantial evidence. Internal evidence.

Shall I set down the rest of the Conjectures which constitute the giant Biography of William Shakespeare? It would strain the Unabridged Dictionary to hold them. He is a Brontosaur: nine bones and six hundred barrels of plaster of paris.

CHAPTER V—"We May Assume"

In the Assuming trade three separate and independent cults are transacting business. Two of these cults are known as the Shakespearites and the Baconians, and I am the other one—the Brontosaurian.

The Shakespearite knows that Shakespeare wrote Shakespeare's Works; the Baconian knows that Francis Bacon wrote them; the Brontosaurian doesn't really know which of them did it, but is quite composedly and contentedly sure that Shakespeare *didn't*, and strongly suspects that Bacon *did*. We all have to do a good deal of assuming, but I am fairly certain that in every case I can call to mind the Baconian assumers have come out ahead of the Shakespearites. Both parties handle the same materials, but the Baconians seem to me to get much more reasonable and rational and persuasive results out of them than is the case with the Shakespearites. The Shakespearite conducts his assuming upon a definite principle, an unchanging and immutable law—which is: 2 and 8 and 7 and 14, added together, make 165. I believe this to be an error. No matter, you cannot get a habit-sodden Shakespearite to cipher-up his materials upon any other basis. With the Baconian it is different. If you place before him the above figures and set him to adding them up, he will never in any case get more than 45 out of them, and in nine cases out of ten he will get just the proper 31.

Let me try to illustrate the two systems in a simple and homely way calculated to bring the idea within the grasp of the ignorant and unintelligent. We will suppose a case: take a lap-bred, house-fed, uneducated, inexperienced kitten; take a rugged old Tom that's scarred from stem to rudder-post with the memorials of strenuous experience, and is so cultured, so educated, so limitlessly erudite that one may say of him "all cat-knowledge is his province"; also, take a mouse. Lock the three up in a holeless, crackless, exitless prison-cell. Wait half an hour, then open the cell, introduce a Shakespearite and a Baconian, and let them cipher and assume. The mouse is missing: the question to be decided is, where is it? You can guess both verdicts beforehand.

One verdict will say the kitten contains the mouse; the other will as certainly say the mouse is in the tomcat.

The Shakespearite will Reason like this—(that is not my word, it is his). He will say the kitten *may have been* attending school when nobody was noticing; therefore *we are warranted in assuming* that it did so; also, it *could have been* training in a court-clerk's office when no one was noticing; since that could have happened, *we are justified in assuming* that it did happen; it *could have studied catology in a garret* when no one was noticing—therefore it *did*; it *could have* attended cat-assizes on the shed-roof nights, for recreation, when no one was noticing, and harvested a knowledge of cat court-forms and cat lawyer-talk in that way: it *could* have done it, therefore without a doubt it did; it could have gone soldiering with a war-tribe when no one was noticing, and learned soldier-wiles and soldier-ways, and what to do with a mouse when opportunity offers; the plain inference, therefore is, that that is what it *did*. Since all these manifold things *could* have occurred, we have *every right to believe* they did occur. These patiently and painstakingly accumulated vast acquirements and competences needed but one thing more—opportunity—to convert themselves into triumphant action. The opportunity came, we have the result; *beyond shadow of question* the mouse is in the kitten.

It is proper to remark that when we of the three cults plant a "*We think we may assume,*" we expect it, under careful watering and fertilizing and tending, to grow up into a strong and hardy and weather-defying "*there isn't a shadow of a doubt*" at last—and it usually happens.

We know what the Baconian's verdict would be: "*There is not a rag of evidence that the kitten has had any training, any education, any experience qualifying it for the present occasion, or is indeed equipped for any achievement above lifting such unclaimed milk as comes its way; but there is abundant evidence—unassailable proof, in fact—that the other animal is equipped, to the last detail, with every qualification necessary for the event. Without shadow of doubt the tomcat contains the mouse.*"

CHAPTER VI

When Shakespeare died, in 1616, great literary productions attributed to him as author had been before the London world and in high favor for twenty-four years. Yet his death was not an event. It made no stir, it attracted no attention. Apparently his eminent literary contemporaries did not realize that a celebrated poet had passed from their midst. Perhaps they knew a play-actor of minor rank had disappeared, but did not regard him as the author of his Works. "We are justified in assuming" this.

His death was not even an event in the little town of Stratford. Does this mean that in Stratford he was not regarded as a celebrity of *any* kind?

"We are privileged to assume"—no, we are indeed *obliged* to assume—that such was the case. He had spent the first twenty-two or twenty-three years of his life there, and of course knew everybody and was known by everybody of that day in the town, including the dogs and the cats and the horses. He had spent the last five or six years of his life there, diligently trading in every big and little thing that had money in it; so we are compelled to assume that many of the folk there in those said latter days knew him personally, and the rest by sight and hearsay. But not as a *celebrity*? Apparently not. For everybody soon forgot to remember any contact with him or any incident connected with him. The dozens of townspeople, still alive, who had known of him or known about him in the first twenty-three years of his life were in the same unremembering condition: if they knew of any incident connected with that period of his life they didn't tell about it. Would they if they had been asked? It is most likely. Were they asked? It is pretty apparent that they were not. Why weren't they? It is a very plausible guess that nobody there or elsewhere was interested to know.

For seven years after Shakespeare's death nobody seems to have been interested in him. Then the quarto was published, and Ben Jonson awoke out of his long indifference and sang a song of praise and put it in the front of the book. Then silence fell *again*.

For sixty years. Then inquiries into Shakespeare's Stratford life began to be made, of Stratfordians. Of Stratfordians who had known Shakespeare or had seen him? No. Then of Stratfordians who had seen people who had known or seen people who had seen Shakespeare? No. Apparently the inquiries were only made of Stratfordians who were not Stratfordians of Shakespeare's day, but later comers; and what they had learned had come to them from persons who had not seen Shakespeare; and what they had learned was not claimed as *fact*, but only as legend—dim and fading and indefinite legend; legend of the calf-slaughtering rank, and not worth remembering either as history or fiction.

Has it ever happened before—or since—that a celebrated person who had spent exactly half of a fairly long life in the village where he was born and reared, was able to slip out of this world and leave that village voiceless and gossipless behind him—utterly voiceless, utterly gossipless? And permanently so? I don't believe it has happened in any case except Shakespeare's. And couldn't and wouldn't have happened in his case if he had been regarded as a celebrity at the time of his death.

When I examine my own case—but let us do that, and see if it will not be recognizable as exhibiting a condition of things quite likely to result, most likely to result, indeed substantially *sure* to result in the case of a celebrated person, a benefactor of the human race. Like me.

My parents brought me to the village of Hannibal, Missouri, on the banks of the Mississippi, when I was two and a half years old. I entered school at five years of age, and drifted from one school to another in the village during nine and a half years. Then my father died, leaving his family in exceedingly straitened circumstances; wherefore my book-education came to a standstill forever, and I became a printer's apprentice, on board and clothes, and when the clothes failed I got a hymn-book in place of them. This for summer wear, probably. I lived in Hannibal fifteen and a half years, altogether, then ran away, according to the custom of persons who are intending to become celebrated. I never lived there afterward. Four years later I became a "cub" on a Mississippi steamboat in the St. Louis and New Orleans trade, and after a year and a half of hard study and hard work the U. S. inspectors rigorously examined me through a couple of long sittings and decided that I knew every inch of the Mississippi—thirteen hundred miles—in the dark and in the day—as well as a baby knows the way to its mother's paps day or night. So they licensed me as a pilot—knighted me, so to speak—and I rose up clothed with authority, a responsible servant of the United States government.

Now then. Shakespeare died young—he was only fifty-two. He had lived in his native village twenty-six years, or about that. He died celebrated (if you believe everything you read in the books). Yet when he died nobody there or elsewhere took any notice of it; and for sixty years afterward no townsman remembered to say anything about him or about his life in Stratford. When the inquirer came at last he got but one fact—no, *legend*—and got that one at second hand, from a person who had only heard it as a rumor, and didn't claim copyright in it as a production of his own. He couldn't, very well, for its date antedated his own birth-date. But necessarily a number of persons were still alive in Stratford who, in the days of their youth, had seen Shakespeare nearly every day in the last five years of his life, and they would have been able to tell that inquirer some first-hand things about him if he had in those last days been a celebrity and therefore a person of interest to the villagers. Why did not the inquirer hunt them up and interview them? Wasn't it worth while? Wasn't the matter of sufficient consequence? Had the inquirer an engagement to see a dog-fight and couldn't spare the time?

It all seems to mean that he never had any literary celebrity, there or elsewhere, and no considerable repute as actor and manager.

Now then, I am away along in life—my seventy-third year being already well behind me—yet *sixteen* of my Hannibal schoolmates are still alive to-day, and can tell—and do tell—inquirers dozens and dozens of incidents of their young lives and mine together; things that happened to us in the morning of life, in the blossom of our youth, in the good days, the dear days, "the days when we went gipsying, a long time ago." Most of them creditable to me, too. One child to whom I paid court when she was five years old and I eight still lives in Hannibal, and she visited me last summer, traversing the necessary ten or twelve hundred miles of railroad without damage to her patience or to her old-young vigor. Another little lassie to whom I paid attention in Hannibal when she was nine years old and I the same, is still alive—in London—and hale and hearty, just as I am. And on the few surviving steamboats—those lingering ghosts and remembrancers of great fleets that plied the big river in the beginning of my water-career—which is exactly as long ago as the whole invoice of the life-years of Shakespeare number—there are still findable two or three river-pilots who saw me do creditable things in those ancient days; and several white-headed engineers; and several roustabouts and mates; and several deck-hands who used to heave the lead for me and send up on the still night air the "six—feet—*scant!*" that made me shudder, and the "*M-a-r-k—twain!*" that took the shudder away, and presently the darling "By the d-e-e-p—four!" that lifted me to heaven for joy. [1] They know about me, and can tell. And so do printers, from St. Louis to New York; and so do newspaper reporters, from Nevada to San Francisco. And so do the police. If Shakespeare had really been celebrated, like me, Stratford could have told things about him; and if my experience goes for anything, they'd have done it.

CHAPTER VII

If I had under my superintendence a controversy appointed to decide whether Shakespeare wrote Shakespeare or not, I believe I would place before the debaters only the one question, *Was Shakespeare ever a practicing lawyer?* and leave everything else out.

It is maintained that the man who wrote the plays was not merely myriad-minded, but also myriad-accomplished: that he not only knew some thousands of things about human life in all its shades and grades, and about the hundred arts and trades and crafts and professions which men busy themselves in, but that he could *talk* about the men and their grades and trades accurately, making no mistakes. Maybe it is so, but have the experts spoken, or is it only Tom, Dick, and Harry? Does the exhibit stand upon wide, and loose, and eloquent generalizing—which is not evidence, and not proof—or upon details, particulars, statistics, illustrations, demonstrations?

Experts of unchallengeable authority have testified definitely as to only one of Shakespeare's multifarious craft-equipments, so far as my recollections of Shakespeare-Bacon talk abide with me—his law-equipment. I do not remember that Wellington or Napoleon ever examined Shakespeare's battles and sieges and strategies, and then decided and established for good and all, that they were militarily flawless; I do not remember that any Nelson, or Drake or Cook ever examined his seamanship and said it showed profound and accurate familiarity with that art; I don't remember that any king or prince or duke has ever testified that Shakespeare was letter-perfect in his handling of royal court-manners and the talk and manners of aristocracies; I don't remember that any illustrious Latinist or Grecian or Frenchman or Spaniard or Italian has proclaimed him a past-master in those languages; I don't remember—well, I don't remember that there is *testimony*—great testimony—imposing testimony—unanswerable and unattackable testimony as to any of Shakespeare's hundred specialties, except one—the law.

Other things change, with time, and the student cannot trace back with certainty the changes that various trades and their processes and technicalities have undergone in the long stretch of a century or two and find out what their processes and technicalities were in those early days, but with the law it is different: it is mile-stoned and documented all the way back, and the master of that wonderful trade, that complex and intricate trade, that awe-compelling trade, has competent ways of knowing whether Shakespeare-law is good law or not; and whether his law-court procedure is correct or not, and whether his legal shop-talk is the shop-talk of a veteran practitioner or only a machine-made counterfeit of it gathered from books and from occasional loiterings in Westminster.

Richard H. Dana served two years before the mast, and had every experience that falls to the lot of the sailor before the mast of our day. His sailor-talk flows from his pen with the sure touch and the ease and confidence of a person who has *lived* what he is talking about, not gathered it from books and random listenings. Hear him:

Having hove short, cast off the gaskets, and made the bunt of each sail fast by the jigger, with a man on each yard, at the word the whole canvas of the ship was loosed, and with the greatest rapidity possible everything was sheeted home and hoisted up, the anchor tripped and cat-headed, and the ship under headway.

Again:

The royal yards were all crossed at once, and royals and sky-sails set, and, as we had the wind free, the booms were run out, and all were aloft, active as cats, laying out on the yards and booms, reeving the studding-sail gear; and sail after sail the captain piled upon her, until she was covered with canvas, her sails looking like a great white cloud resting upon a black speck.

Once more. A race in the Pacific:

Our antagonist was in her best trim. Being clear of the point, the breeze became stiff, and the royal-masts bent under our sails, but we would not take them in until we saw three boys spring into the rigging of the *California*; then they were all furled at once, but with orders to our boys to stay aloft at the top-gallant mast-heads and loose them again at the word. It was my duty to furl the fore-royal; and while standing by to loose it again, I had a fine view of the scene. From where I stood, the two vessels seemed nothing but spars and sails, while their narrow decks, far below, slanting over by the force of the wind aloft, appeared hardly capable of supporting the great fabrics raised upon them. The *California* was to windward of us, and had every advantage; yet, while the breeze was stiff we held our own. As soon as it began to slacken she ranged a little ahead, and the order was given to loose the royals. In an instant the gaskets were off and the bunt dropped. "Sheet home the fore-royal!"—"Weather sheet's home!"—"Lee sheet's home!"—"Hoist away, sir!" is bawled from aloft. "Overhaul your clewlines!" shouts the mate. "Aye-aye, sir, all clear!"—"Taut leech! belay! Well the lee brace; haul taut to windward!" and the royals are set.

What would the captain of any sailing-vessel of our time say to that? He would say, "The man that wrote that didn't learn his trade out of a book, he has *been* there!" But would this same captain be competent to sit in judgment upon Shakespeare's seamanship—considering the changes in ships and ship-talk that have necessarily taken place, unrecorded, unremembered, and lost to history in the last three hundred years? It is my conviction that Shakespeare's sailor-talk would be Choctaw to him. For instance—from *The Tempest*:

Master. Boatswain!

Boatswain. Here, master; what cheer?

Master. Good, speak to the mariners: fall to't, yarely, or we run ourselves to ground; bestir, bestir!

(*Enter mariners.*)

Boatswain. Heigh, my hearts! cheerly, cheerly, my hearts! yare, yare! Take in the topsail. Tend to the master's whistle . . . Down with the topmast! yare! lower, lower! Bring her to try wi' the main course . . . Lay her a-hold, a-hold! Set her two courses. Off to sea again; lay her off.

That will do, for the present; let us yare a little, now, for a change.

If a man should write a book and in it make one of his characters say, "Here, devil, empty the quoins into the standing galley and the imposing stone into the hell-box; assemble the comps around the frisket and let them jeff for takes and be quick about it," I should recognize a mistake or two in the phrasing, and would know that the writer was only a printer theoretically, not practically.

I have been a quartz miner in the silver regions—a pretty hard life; I know all the palaver of that business: I know all about discovery claims and the subordinate claims; I know all about lodes, ledges, outcroppings, dips, spurs, angles, shafts, drifts, inclines, levels, tunnels, air-shafts, "horses," clay casings, granite casings; quartz mills and their batteries; arastras, and how to charge them with quicksilver and sulphate of copper; and how to clean them up, and how to reduce the resulting amalgam in the retorts, and how to cast the bullion into pigs; and finally I know how to screen tailings, and also how to hunt for something less robust to do, and find it. I know the *argot* of the quartz-mining and milling industry familiarly; and so whenever Bret Harte introduces that industry into a story, the first time one of his miners opens his mouth I recognize from his phrasing that Harte got the phrasing by listening—like Shakespeare—I mean the Stratford one—not by experience. No one can talk the quartz dialect correctly without learning it with pick and shovel and drill and fuse.

I have been a surface-miner—gold—and I know all its mysteries, and the dialect that belongs with them; and whenever Harte introduces that industry into a story I know by the phrasing of his characters that neither he nor they have ever served that trade.

I have been a "pocket" miner—a sort of gold mining not findable in any but one little spot in the world, so far as I know. I know how, with horn and water, to find the trail of a pocket and trace it step by step and stage by stage up the mountain to its source, and find the compact little nest of yellow metal reposing in its secret home under the ground. I know the language of that trade, that capricious trade, that fascinating buried-treasure trade, and can catch any writer who tries to use it without having learned it by the sweat of his brow and the labor of his hands.

I know several other trades and the *argot* that goes with them; and whenever a person tries to talk the talk peculiar to any of them without having learned it at its source I can trap him always before he gets far on his road.

And so, as I have already remarked, if I were required to superintend a Bacon-Shakespeare controversy, I would narrow the matter down to a single question—the only one, so far as the previous controversies have informed me, concerning which illustrious experts of unimpeachable competency have testified: *Was the author of Shakespeare's Works a lawyer?*—a lawyer deeply read and of limitless experience? I would put aside the guesses, and surmises, and perhapses, and might-have-beens, and could-have beens, and must-have-beens, and we-are justified-in-presumings, and the rest of those vague spectres and shadows and indefinitenesses, and stand or fall, win or lose, by the verdict rendered by the jury upon that single question. If the verdict was Yes, I should feel quite convinced that the Stratford Shakespeare, the actor, manager, and trader who died so obscure, so forgotten, so destitute of even village consequence that sixty years afterward no fellow-citizen and friend of his later days remembered to tell anything about him, did not write the Works.

Chapter XIII of *The Shakespeare Problem Restated* bears the heading "Shakespeare as a Lawyer," and comprises some fifty pages of expert testimony, with comments thereon, and I will copy the first nine, as being sufficient all by themselves, as it seems to me, to settle the question which I have conceived to be the master-key to the Shakespeare-Bacon puzzle.

CHAPTER VIII—Shakespeare as a Lawyer [2]

The Plays and Poems of Shakespeare supply ample evidence that their author not only had a very extensive and accurate knowledge of law, but that he was well acquainted with the manners and customs of members of the Inns of Court and with legal life generally.

"While novelists and dramatists are constantly making mistakes as to the laws of marriage, of wills, and inheritance, to Shakespeare's law, lavishly as he expounds it, there can neither be demurrer, nor bill of exceptions, nor writ of error." Such was the testimony borne by one of the most distinguished lawyers of the nineteenth century who was raised to the high office of Lord Chief Justice in 1850, and subsequently became Lord Chancellor. Its weight will, doubtless, be more appreciated by lawyers than by laymen, for only lawyers know how impossible it is for those who have not served an apprenticeship to the law to avoid displaying their ignorance if they venture to employ legal terms and to discuss legal doctrines. "There is nothing so dangerous," wrote Lord Campbell, "as for one not of the craft to tamper with our freemasonry." A layman is certain to betray himself by using some expression which a lawyer would never employ. Mr. Sidney Lee himself supplies us with an example of this. He writes (p. 164): "On February 15, 1609, Shakespeare . . . obtained judgment from a jury against Addenbroke for the payment of No. 6, and No. 1. 5s. 0d. costs." Now a lawyer would never have spoken of obtaining "judgment from a jury," for it is the function of a jury not to deliver judgment (which is the prerogative of the court), but to find a verdict on the facts. The error is, indeed, a venial one, but it is just one of those little things which at once enable a lawyer to know if the writer is a layman or "one of the craft."

But when a layman ventures to plunge deeply into legal subjects, he is naturally apt to make an exhibition of his incompetence. "Let a non-professional man, however acute," writes Lord Campbell again, "presume to talk law, or to draw illustrations from legal science in discussing other subjects, and he will speedily fall into laughable absurdity."

And what does the same high authority say about Shakespeare? He had "a deep technical knowledge of the law," and an easy familiarity with "some of the most abstruse proceedings in English jurisprudence." And again: "Whenever he indulges this propensity he uniformly lays down good law." Of *Henry IV.*, Part 2, he says: "If Lord Eldon could be supposed to have written the play, I do not see how he could be chargeable with having forgotten any of his law while writing it." Charles and Mary Cowden Clarke speak of "the marvelous intimacy which he displays with legal terms, his frequent adoption of them in illustration, and his curiously technical knowledge of their form and force." Malone, himself a lawyer, wrote: "His knowledge of legal terms is not merely such as might be acquired by the casual observation of even his all-comprehending mind; it has the appearance of technical skill." Another lawyer and well-known Shakespearean, Richard Grant White, says: "No dramatist of the time, not even Beaumont, who was the younger son of a judge of the Common Pleas, and who after studying in the Inns of Court abandoned law for the drama, used legal phrases with Shakespeare's readiness and exactness. And the significance of this fact is heightened by another, that it is only to the language of the law that he exhibits this inclination. The phrases peculiar to other occupations serve him on rare occasions by way of description, comparison or illustration, generally when something in the scene suggests them, but legal phrases flow from his pen as part of his vocabulary, and parcel of his thought. Take the word 'purchase' for instance, which, in ordinary use, means to acquire by giving value, but applies in law to all legal modes of obtaining property except by inheritance or descent, and in this peculiar sense the word occurs five times in Shakespeare's thirty-four plays, and only in one single instance in the fifty-four plays of Beaumont and Fletcher. It has been suggested that it was in attendance upon the courts in London that he picked up his legal vocabulary. But this supposition not only fails to account for Shakespeare's peculiar freedom and exactness in the use of that phraseology, it does not even place him in the way of learning those terms his use of which is most remarkable, which are not such as he would have heard at ordinary proceedings at *nisi prius*, but such as refer to the tenure or transfer of real property, 'fine and recovery,' 'statutes merchant,' 'purchase,' 'indenture,' 'tenure,' 'double voucher,' 'fee simple,' 'fee farm,' 'remainder,' 'reversion,' 'forfeiture,' etc. This conveyancer's jargon could not have been picked up by hanging round the courts of law in London two hundred and fifty years ago, when suits as to the title of real property were comparatively rare. And beside, Shakespeare uses his law just as freely in his first plays, written in his first London years, as in those produced at a later period. Just as exactly, too; for the correctness and propriety with which these terms are introduced have compelled the admiration of a Chief Justice and a Lord Chancellor."

Senator Davis wrote: "We seem to have something more than a sciolist's temerity of indulgence in the terms of an unfamiliar art. No legal solecisms will be found. The abstrusest elements of the common law are impressed into a disciplined service. Over and over again, where such knowledge is unexampled in writers unlearned in the law, Shakespeare appears in perfect possession of it. In the law of real property, its rules of tenure and descents, its entails, its fines and recoveries, their vouchers and double vouchers, in the procedure of the Courts, the method of bringing writs and arrests, the nature of actions, the rules of pleading, the law of escapes and of contempt of court, in the principles of evidence, both technical and philosophical, in the distinction between the temporal and spiritual tribunals, in the law of attainder and forfeiture, in the requisites of a valid marriage, in the presumption of legitimacy, in the learning of the law of prerogative, in the inalienable character of the Crown, this mastership appears with surprising authority."

To all this testimony (and there is much more which I have not cited) may now be added that of a great lawyer of our own times, *viz.*: Sir James Plaisted Wilde, Q.C. created a Baron of the Exchequer in 1860, promoted to the post of Judge-Ordinary and Judge of the Courts of Probate and Divorce in 1863, and better known to the world as Lord Penzance, to which dignity he was raised in 1869. Lord Penzance, as all lawyers know, and as the late Mr. Inderwick, K.C., has testified, was one of the first legal authorities of his day, famous for his "remarkable grasp of legal principles," and "endowed by nature with a remarkable facility for marshalling facts, and for a clear expression of his views."

Lord Penzance speaks of Shakespeare's "perfect familiarity with not only the principles, axioms, and maxims, but the technicalities of English law, a knowledge so perfect and intimate that he was never incorrect and never at fault . . . The mode in which this knowledge was pressed into service on all occasions to express his meaning and illustrate his thoughts, was quite unexampled. He seems to have had a special pleasure in his complete and ready mastership of it in all its branches. As manifested in the plays, this legal knowledge and learning had therefore a special character which places it on a wholly different footing from the rest of the multifarious knowledge which is exhibited in page after page of the plays. At every turn and point at which the author required a metaphor, simile, or illustration, his mind ever turned *first* to the law. He seems almost to have *thought* in legal phrases, the commonest of legal expressions were ever at the end of his pen in description or illustration. That he should have descanted in lawyer language when he had a forensic subject in hand, such as Shylock's bond, was to be expected, but the knowledge of law in 'Shakespeare' was exhibited in a far different manner: it protruded itself on all occasions, appropriate or inappropriate, and mingled itself with strains of thought widely divergent from forensic subjects." Again: "To acquire a perfect familiarity with legal principles, and an accurate and ready use of the technical terms and phrases not only of the conveyancer's office but of the pleader's chambers and the Courts at Westminster, nothing short of employment in some career involving constant contact with legal questions and general legal work would be requisite. But a continuous employment involves the element of time, and time was just what the manager of two theatres had not at his disposal. In what portion of Shakespeare's (*i.e.* Shakspere's) career would it be possible to point out that time could be found for the interposition of a legal employment in the chambers or offices of practising lawyers?"

Stratfordians, as is well known, casting about for some possible explanation of Shakespeare's extraordinary knowledge of law, have made the suggestion that Shakespeare might, conceivably, have been a clerk in an attorney's office before he came to London. Mr. Collier wrote to Lord Campbell to ask his opinion as to the probability of this being true. His answer was as follows: "You require us to believe implicitly a fact, of which, if true, positive and irrefragable evidence in his own handwriting might have been forthcoming to establish it. Not having been actually enrolled as an attorney, neither the records of the local court at Stratford nor of the superior Courts at Westminster would present his name as being concerned in any suit as an attorney, but it might reasonably have been expected that there would be deeds or wills witnessed by him still extant, and after a very diligent search none such can be discovered."

Upon this Lord Penzance comments: "It cannot be doubted that Lord Campbell was right in this. No young man could have been at work in an attorney's office without being called upon continually to act as a witness, and in many other ways leaving traces of his work and name." There is not a single fact or incident in all that is known of Shakespeare, even by rumor or tradition, which supports this notion of a clerkship. And after much argument and surmise which has been indulged in on this subject, we may, I think, safely put the notion on one side, for no less an authority than Mr. Grant White says finally that the idea of his having been clerk to an attorney has been "blown to pieces."

It is altogether characteristic of Mr. Churton Collins that he, nevertheless, adopts this exploded myth. "That Shakespeare was in early life employed as a clerk in an attorney's office, may be correct. At Stratford there was by royal charter a Court of Record sitting every fortnight, with six attorneys, beside the town clerk, belonging to it, and it is certainly not straining probability to suppose that the young Shakespeare may have had employment in one of them. There is, it is true, no tradition to this effect, but such traditions as we have about Shakespeare's occupation between the time of leaving school and going to London are so loose and baseless that no confidence can be placed in them. It is, to say the least, more probable that he was in an attorney's office than that he was a butcher killing calves 'in a high style,' and making speeches over them."

This is a charming specimen of Stratfordian argument. There is, as we have seen, a very old tradition that Shakespeare was a butcher's apprentice. John Dowdall, who made a tour in Warwickshire in 1693, testifies to it as coming from the old clerk who showed him over the church, and it is unhesitatingly accepted as true by Mr. Halliwell-Phillipps. (Vol I, p. 11, and see Vol. II, p. 71, 72.) Mr. Sidney Lee sees nothing improbable in it, and it is supported by Aubrey, who must have written his account some time before 1680, when his manuscript was completed. Of the attorney's clerk hypothesis, on the other hand, there is not the faintest vestige of a tradition. It has been evolved out of the fertile imaginations of embarrassed Stratfordians, seeking for some explanation of the Stratford rustic's marvellous acquaintance with law and legal terms and legal life. But Mr. Churton Collins has not the least hesitation in throwing over the tradition which has the warrant of antiquity and setting up in its stead this ridiculous invention, for which not only is there no shred of positive evidence, but which, as Lord Campbell and Lord Penzance point out, is really put out of court by the negative evidence, since "no young man could have been at work in an attorney's office without being called upon continually to act as a witness, and in many other ways leaving traces of his work and name." And as Mr. Edwards further points out, since the day when Lord Campbell's book was published (between forty and fifty years ago), "every old deed or will, to say nothing of other legal papers, dated during the period of William Shakespeare's youth, has been scrutinized over half a dozen shires, and not one signature of the young man has been found."

Moreover, if Shakespeare had served as clerk in an attorney's office it is clear that he must have so served for a considerable period in order to have gained (if indeed it is credible that he could have so gained) his remarkable knowledge of law. Can we then for a moment believe that, if this had been so, tradition would have been absolutely silent on the matter? That Dowdall's old clerk, over eighty years of age, should have never heard of it (though he was sure enough about the butcher's apprentice), and that all the other ancient witnesses should be in similar ignorance!

But such are the methods of Stratfordian controversy. Tradition is to be scouted when it is found inconvenient, but cited as irrefragable truth when it suits the case. Shakespeare of Stratford was the author of the *Plays* and *Poems*, but the author of the *Plays* and *Poems* could not have been a butcher's apprentice. Away, therefore, with tradition. But the author of the *Plays* and *Poems must* have had a very large and a very accurate knowledge of the law. Therefore, Shakespeare of Stratford must have been an attorney's clerk! The method is simplicity itself. By similar reasoning Shakespeare has been made a country schoolmaster, a soldier, a physician, a printer, and a good many other things beside, according to the inclination and the exigencies of the commentator. It would not be in the least surprising to find that he was studying Latin as a schoolmaster and law in an attorney's office at the same time.

However, we must do Mr. Collins the justice of saying that he has fully recognized, what is indeed tolerably obvious, that Shakespeare must have had a sound legal training. "It may, of course, be urged," he writes, "that Shakespeare's knowledge of medicine, and particularly that branch of it which related to morbid psychology, is equally remarkable, and that no one has ever contended that he was a physician. (Here Mr. Collins is wrong; that contention also has been put forward.) It may be urged that his acquaintance with the technicalities of other crafts and callings, notably of marine and military affairs, was also extraordinary, and yet no one has suspected him of being a sailor or a soldier. (Wrong again. Why even Messrs. Garnett and Gosse 'suspect' that he was a soldier!) This may be conceded, but the concession hardly furnishes an analogy. To these and all other subjects he recurs occasionally, and in season, but with reminiscences of the law his memory, as is abundantly clear, was simply saturated. In season and out of season now in manifest, now in recondite application, he presses it into the service of expression and illustration. At least a third of his myriad metaphors are derived from it. It would indeed be difficult to find a single act in any of his dramas, nay, in some of them, a single scene, the diction and imagery of which is not colored by it. Much of his law may have been acquired from three books easily accessible to him, namely Tottell's *Precedents* (1572), Pulton's *Statutes* (1578), and Fraunce's *Lawier's Logike* (1588), works with which he certainly seems to have been familiar; but much of it could only have come from one who had an intimate acquaintance with legal proceedings. We quite agree with Mr. Castle that Shakespeare's legal knowledge is not what could have been picked up in an attorney's office, but could only have been learned by an actual attendance at the Courts, at a Pleader's Chambers, and on circuit, or by associating intimately with members of the Bench and Bar."

This is excellent. But what is Mr. Collins' explanation. "Perhaps the simplest solution of the problem is to accept the hypothesis that in early life he was in an attorney's office (!), that he there contracted a love for the law which never left him, that as a young man in London, he continued to study or dabble in it for his amusement, to stroll in leisure hours into the Courts, and to frequent the society of lawyers. On no other supposition is it possible to explain the attraction which the law evidently had for him, and his minute and undeviating accuracy in a subject where no layman who has indulged in such copious and ostentatious display of legal technicalities has ever yet succeeded in keeping himself from tripping."

A lame conclusion. "No other supposition" indeed! Yes, there is another, and a very obvious supposition, namely, that Shakespeare was himself a lawyer, well versed in his trade, versed in all the ways of the courts, and living in close intimacy with judges and members of the Inns of Court.

One is, of course, thankful that Mr. Collins has appreciated the fact that Shakespeare must have had a sound legal training, but I may be forgiven if I do not attach quite so much importance to his pronouncements on this branch of the subject as to those of Malone, Lord Campbell, Judge Holmes, Mr. Castle, K.C., Lord Penzance, Mr. Grant White, and other lawyers, who have expressed their opinion on the matter of Shakespeare's legal acquirements.

Here it may, perhaps, be worth while to quote again from Lord Penzance's book as to the suggestion that Shakespeare had somehow or other managed "to acquire a perfect familiarity with legal principles, and an accurate and ready use of the technical terms and phrases, not only of the conveyancer's office, but of the pleader's chambers and the courts at Westminster." This, as Lord Penzance points out, "would require nothing short of employment in some career involving *constant contact* with legal questions and general legal work." But "in what portion of Shakespeare's career would it be possible to point out that time could be found for the interposition of a legal employment in the chambers or offices of practising lawyers? . . . It is beyond doubt that at an early period he was called upon to abandon his attendance at school and assist his father, and was soon after, at the age of sixteen, bound apprentice to a trade. While under the obligation of this bond he could not have pursued any other employment. Then he leaves Stratford and comes to London. He has to provide himself with the means of a livelihood, and this he did in some capacity at the theatre. No one doubts that. The holding of horses is scouted by many, and perhaps with justice, as being unlikely and certainly unproved; but whatever the nature of his employment was at the theatre, there is hardly room for the belief that it could have been other than continuous, for his progress there was so rapid. Ere long he had been taken into the company as an actor, and was soon spoken of as a 'Johannes Factotum.' His rapid accumulation of wealth speaks volumes for the constancy and activity of his services. One fails to see when there could be a break in the current of his life at this period of it, giving room or opportunity for legal or indeed any other employment. 'In 1589,' says Knight, 'we have undeniable evidence that he had not only a casual engagement, was not only a salaried servant, as many players were, but was a shareholder in the company of the Queen's players with other shareholders below him on the list.' This (1589) would be within two years after his arrival in London, which is placed by White and Halliwell-Phillipps about the year 1587. The difficulty in supposing that, starting with a state of ignorance in 1587, when he is supposed to have come to London, he was induced to enter upon a course of most extended study and mental culture, is almost insuperable. Still it was physically possible, provided always that he could have had access to the needful books. But this legal training seems to me to stand on a different footing. It is not only unaccountable and incredible, but it is actually negatived by the known facts of his career." Lord Penzance then refers to the fact that "by 1592 (according to the best authority, Mr. Grant White) several of the plays had been written. *The Comedy of Errors* in 1589, *Love's Labour's Lost* in 1589, *Two Gentlemen of Verona* in 1589 or 1590, and so forth," and then asks, "with this catalogue of dramatic work on hand . . . was it possible that he could have taken a leading part in the management and conduct of two theatres, and if Mr. Phillipps is to be relied upon, taken his share in the performances of the provincial tours of his company—and at the same time devoted himself to the study of the law in all its branches so efficiently as to make himself complete master of its principles and practice, and saturate his mind with all its most technical terms?"

I have cited this passage from Lord Penzance's book, because it lay before me, and I had already quoted from it on the matter of Shakespeare's legal knowledge; but other writers have still better set forth the insuperable difficulties, as they seem to me, which beset the idea that Shakespeare might have found time in some unknown period of early life, amid multifarious other occupations, for the study of classics, literature and law, to say nothing of languages and a few other matters. Lord Penzance further asks his readers: "Did you ever meet with or hear of an instance in which a young man in this country gave himself up to legal studies and engaged in legal employments, which is the only way of becoming familiar with the technicalities of practice, unless with the view of practicing in that profession? I do not believe that it would be easy, or indeed possible, to produce an instance in which the law has been seriously studied in all its branches, except as a qualification for practice in the legal profession."

* * * * *

This testimony is so strong, so direct, so authoritative; and so uncheapened, unwatered by guesses, and surmises, and maybe-so's, and might-have-beens, and could-have-beens, and must-have-beens, and the rest of that ton of plaster of paris out of which the biographers have built the colossal brontosaur which goes by the Stratford actor's name, that it quite convinces me that the man who wrote Shakespeare's Works knew all about law and lawyers. Also, that that man could not have been the Stratford Shakespeare—and *wasn't*.

Who did write these Works, then?

I wish I knew.

CHAPTER IX

Did Francis Bacon write Shakespeare's Works?

Nobody knows.

We cannot say we *know* a thing when that thing has not been proved. *Know* is too strong a word to use when the evidence is not final and absolutely conclusive. We can infer, if we want to, like those slaves . . . No, I will not write that word, it is not kind, it is not courteous. The upholders of the Stratford-Shakespeare superstition call *us* the hardest names they can think of, and they keep doing it all the time; very well, if they like to descend to that level, let them do it, but I will not so undignify myself as to follow them. I cannot call them harsh names; the most I can do is to indicate them by terms reflecting my disapproval; and this without malice, without venom.

To resume. What I was about to say, was, those thugs have built their entire superstition upon *inferences*, not upon known and established facts. It is a weak method, and poor, and I am glad to be able to say our side never resorts to it while there is anything else to resort to.

But when we must, we must; and we have now arrived at a place of that sort.

Since the Stratford Shakespeare couldn't have written the Works, we infer that somebody did. Who was it, then? This requires some more inferring.

Ordinarily when an unsigned poem sweeps across the continent like a tidal wave, whose roar and boom and thunder are made up of admiration, delight and applause, a dozen obscure people rise up and claim the authorship. Why a dozen, instead of only one or two? One reason is, because there's a dozen that are recognizably competent to do that poem. Do you remember "Beautiful Snow"? Do you remember "Rock Me to Sleep, Mother, Rock Me to Sleep"? Do you remember "Backward, turn backward, O Time, in thy flight! Make me a child again just for to-night"? I remember them very well. Their authorship was claimed by most of the grown-up people who were alive at the time, and every claimant had one plausible argument in his favor, at least: to wit, he could have done the authoring; he was competent.

Have the Works been claimed by a dozen? They haven't. There was good reason. The world knows there was but one man on the planet at the time who was competent—not a dozen, and not two. A long time ago the dwellers in a far country used now and then to find a procession of prodigious footprints stretching across the plain—footprints that were three miles apart, each footprint a third of a mile long and a furlong deep, and with forests and villages mashed to mush in it. Was there any doubt as to who had made that mighty trail? Were there a dozen claimants? Were there two? No— the people knew who it was that had been along there: there was only one Hercules.

There has been only one Shakespeare. There couldn't be two; certainly there couldn't be two at the same time. It takes ages to bring forth a Shakespeare, and some more ages to match him. This one was not matched before his time; nor during his time; and hasn't been matched since. The prospect of matching him in our time is not bright.

The Baconians claim that the Stratford Shakespeare was not qualified to write the Works, and that Francis Bacon was. They claim that Bacon possessed the stupendous equipment—both natural and acquired—for the miracle; and that no other Englishman of his day possessed the like; or, indeed, anything closely approaching it.

Macaulay, in his Essay, has much to say about the splendor and horizonless magnitude of that equipment. Also, he has synopsized Bacon's history: a thing which cannot be done for the Stratford Shakespeare, for he hasn't any history to synopsize. Bacon's history is open to the world, from his boyhood to his death in old age—a history consisting of known facts, displayed in minute and multitudinous detail; *facts*, not guesses and conjectures and might-have-beens.

Whereby it appears that he was born of a race of statesmen, and had a Lord Chancellor for his father, and a mother who was "distinguished both as a linguist and a theologian: she corresponded in Greek with Bishop Jewell, and translated his *Apologia* from the Latin so correctly that neither he nor Archbishop Parker could suggest a single alteration." It is the atmosphere we are reared in that determines how our inclinations and aspirations shall tend. The atmosphere furnished by the parents to the son in this present case was an atmosphere saturated with learning; with thinkings and ponderings upon deep subjects; and with polite culture. It had its natural effect. Shakespeare of Stratford was reared in a house which had no use for books, since its owners, his parents, were without education. This may have had an effect upon the son, but we do not know, because we have no history of him of an informing sort. There were but few books anywhere, in that day, and only the well-to-do and highly educated possessed them, they being almost confined to the dead languages. "All the valuable books then extant in all the vernacular dialects of Europe would hardly have filled a single shelf"—imagine it! The few existing books were in the Latin tongue mainly. "A person who was ignorant of it was shut out from all acquaintance—not merely with Cicero and Virgil, but with the most interesting memoirs, state papers, and pamphlets of his own time"—a literature necessary to the Stratford lad, for his fictitious reputation's sake, since the writer of his Works would begin to use it wholesale and in a most masterly way before the lad was hardly more than out of his teens and into his twenties.

At fifteen Bacon was sent to the university, and he spent three years there. Thence he went to Paris in the train of the English Ambassador, and there he mingled daily with the wise, the cultured, the great, and the aristocracy of fashion, during another three years. A total of six years spent at the sources of knowledge; knowledge both of books and of men. The three spent at the university were coeval with the second and last three spent by the little Stratford lad at Stratford school supposedly, and perhapsedly, and maybe, and by inference—with nothing to infer from. The second three of the Baconian six were "presumably" spent by the Stratford lad as apprentice to a butcher. That is, the thugs presume it—on no evidence of any kind. Which is their way, when they want a historical fact. Fact and presumption are, for business purposes, all the same to them. They know the difference, but they also know how to blink it. They know, too, that while in history-building a fact is better than a presumption, it doesn't take a presumption long to bloom into a fact when *they* have the handling of it. They know by old experience that when they get hold of a presumption-tadpole he is not going to *stay* tadpole in their history-tank; no, they know how to develop him into the giant four-legged bullfrog of *fact*, and make him sit up on his hams, and puff out his chin, and look important and insolent and come-to-stay; and assert his genuine simon-pure authenticity with a thundering bellow that will convince everybody because it is so loud. The thug is aware that loudness convinces sixty persons where reasoning convinces but one. I wouldn't be a thug, not even if—but never mind about that, it has nothing to do with the argument, and it is not noble in spirit besides. If I am better than a thug, is the merit mine? No, it is His. Then to Him be the praise. That is the right spirit.

They "presume" the lad severed his "presumed" connection with the Stratford school to become apprentice to a butcher. They also "presume" that the butcher was his father. They don't know. There is no written record of it, nor any other actual evidence. If it would have helped their case any, they would have apprenticed him to thirty butchers, to fifty butchers, to a wilderness of butchers—all by their patented method "presumption." If it will help their case they will do it yet; and if it will further help it, they will "presume" that all those butchers were his father. And the week after, they will *say* it. Why, it is just like being the past tense of the compound reflexive adverbial incandescent hypodermic irregular accusative Noun of Multitude; which is father to the expression which the grammarians call Verb. It is like a whole ancestry, with only one posterity.

To resume. Next, the young Bacon took up the study of law, and mastered that abstruse science. From that day to the end of his life he was daily in close contact with lawyers and judges; not as a casual onlooker in intervals between holding horses in front of a theatre, but as a practicing lawyer—a great and successful one, a renowned one, a Launcelot of the bar, the most formidable lance in the high brotherhood of the legal Table Round; he lived in the law's atmosphere thenceforth, all his years, and by sheer ability forced his way up its difficult steeps to its supremest summit, the Lord Chancellorship, leaving behind him no fellow craftsman qualified to challenge his divine right to that majestic place.

When we read the praises bestowed by Lord Penzance and the other illustrious experts upon the legal condition and legal aptnesses, brilliances, profundities and felicities so prodigally displayed in the Plays, and try to fit them to the history-less Stratford stage-manager, they sound wild, strange, incredible, ludicrous; but when we put them in the mouth of Bacon they do not sound strange, they seem in their natural and rightful place, they seem at home there. Please turn back and read them again. Attributed to Shakespeare of Stratford they are meaningless, they are inebriate extravagancies— intemperate admirations of the dark side of the moon, so to speak; attributed to Bacon, they are admirations of the golden glories of the moon's front side, the moon at the full—and not intemperate, not overwrought, but sane and right, and justified. "At every turn and point at which the author required a metaphor, simile or illustration, his mind ever turned *first* to the law; he seems almost to have *thought* in legal phrases; the commonest legal phrases, the commonest of legal expressions were ever at the end of his pen." That could happen to no one but a person whose *trade* was the law; it could not happen to a dabbler in it. Veteran mariners fill their conversation with sailor-phrases and draw all their similes from the ship and the sea and the storm, but no mere *passenger* ever does it, be he of Stratford or elsewhere; or could do it with anything resembling accuracy, if he were hardy enough to try. Please read again what Lord Campbell and the other great authorities have said about Bacon when they thought they were saying it about Shakespeare of Stratford.

CHAPTER X—The Rest of the Equipment

The author of the Plays was equipped, beyond every other man of his time, with wisdom, erudition, imagination, capaciousness of mind, grace and majesty of expression. Every one has said it, no one doubts it. Also, he had humor, humor in rich abundance, and always wanting to break out. We have no evidence of any kind that Shakespeare of Stratford possessed any of these gifts or any of these acquirements. The only lines he ever wrote, so far as we know, are substantially barren of them—barren of all of them.

> Good friend for Iesus sake forbeare
>
> To digg the dust encloased heare:
>
> Blest be ye man yt spares thes stones
>
> And curst be he yt moves my bones.

Ben Jonson says of Bacon, as orator:

His language, *where he could spare and pass by a jest*, was nobly censorious. No man ever spoke more neatly, more pressly, more weightily, or suffered less emptiness, less idleness, in what he uttered. No member of his speech but consisted of his (its) own graces . . . The fear of every man that heard him was lest he should make an end.

From Macaulay:

He continued to distinguish himself in Parliament, particularly by his exertions in favor of one excellent measure on which the King's heart was set—the union of England and Scotland. It was not difficult for such an intellect to discover many irresistible arguments in favor of such a scheme. He conducted the great case of the *Post Nati* in the Exchequer Chamber; and the decision of the judges—a decision the legality of which may be questioned, but the beneficial effect of which must be acknowledged—was in a great measure attributed to his dexterous management.

Again:

While actively engaged in the House of Commons and in the courts of law, he still found leisure for letters and philosophy. The noble treatise on the *Advancement of Learning*, which at a later period was expanded into the *De Augmentis*, appeared in 1605.

The *Wisdom of the Ancients*, a work which if it had proceeded from any other writer would have been considered as a masterpiece of wit and learning, was printed in 1609.

In the meantime the *Novum Organum* was slowly proceeding. Several distinguished men of learning had been permitted to see portions of that extraordinary book, and they spoke with the greatest admiration of his genius.

Even Sir Thomas Bodley, after perusing the *Cogitata et Visa*, one of the most precious of those scattered leaves out of which the great oracular volume was afterward made up, acknowledged that "in all proposals and plots in that book, Bacon showed himself a master workman"; and that "it could not be gainsaid but all the treatise over did abound with choice conceits of the present state of learning, and with worthy contemplations of the means to procure it."

In 1612 a new edition of the *Essays* appeared, with additions surpassing the original collection both in bulk and quality.

Nor did these pursuits distract Bacon's attention from a work the most arduous, the most glorious, and the most useful that even his mighty powers could have achieved, "the reducing and recompiling," to use his own phrase, "of the laws of England."

To serve the exacting and laborious offices of Attorney General and Solicitor General would have satisfied the appetite of any other man for hard work, but Bacon had to add the vast literary industries just described, to satisfy his. He was a born worker.

The service which he rendered to letters during the last five years of his life, amid ten thousand distractions and vexations, increase the regret with which we think on the many years which he had wasted, to use the words of Sir Thomas Bodley, "on such study as was not worthy such a student."

He commenced a digest of the laws of England, a History of England under the Princes of the House of Tudor, a body of National History, a Philosophical Romance. He made extensive and valuable additions to his Essays. He published the inestimable *Treatise De Argumentis Scientiarum*.

Did these labors of Hercules fill up his time to his contentment, and quiet his appetite for work? Not entirely:

The trifles with which he amused himself in hours of pain and languor bore the mark of his mind. *The best jestbook in the world* is that which he dictated from memory, without referring to any book, on a day on which illness had rendered him incapable of serious study.

Here are some scattered remarks (from Macaulay) which throw light upon Bacon, and seem to indicate—and maybe demonstrate—that he was competent to write the Plays and Poems:

With great minuteness of observation he had an amplitude of comprehension such as has never yet been vouchsafed to any other human being.

The "Essays" contain abundant proofs that no nice feature of character, no peculiarity in the ordering of a house, a garden or a court-masque, could escape the notice of one whose mind was capable of taking in the whole world of knowledge.

His understanding resembled the tent which the fairy Paribanou gave to Prince Ahmed: fold it, and it seemed a toy for the hand of a lady; spread it, and the armies of powerful Sultans might repose beneath its shade.

The knowledge in which Bacon excelled all men was a knowledge of the mutual relations of all departments of knowledge.

In a letter written when he was only thirty-one, to his uncle, Lord Burleigh, he said, "I have taken all knowledge to be my province."

Though Bacon did not arm his philosophy with the weapons of logic, he adorned her profusely with all the richest decorations of rhetoric.

The practical faculty was powerful in Bacon; but not, like his wit, so powerful as occasionally to usurp the place of his reason, and to tyrannize over the whole man.

There are too many places in the Plays where this happens. Poor old dying John of Gaunt volleying second-rate puns at his own name, is a pathetic instance of it. "We may assume" that it is Bacon's fault, but the Stratford Shakespeare has to bear the blame.

No imagination was ever at once so strong and so thoroughly subjugated. It stopped at the first check from good sense.

In truth much of Bacon's life was passed in a visionary world—amid things as strange as any that are described in the "Arabian Tales" . . . amid buildings more sumptuous than the palace of Aladdin, fountains more wonderful than the golden water of Parizade, conveyances more rapid than the hippogryph of Ruggiero, arms more formidable than the lance of Astolfo, remedies more efficacious than the balsam of Fierabras. Yet in his magnificent day-dreams there was nothing wild—nothing but what sober reason sanctioned.

Bacon's greatest performance is the first book of the *Novum Organum* . . . Every part of it blazes with wit, but with wit which is employed only to illustrate and decorate truth. No book ever made so great a revolution in the mode of thinking, overthrew so many prejudices, introduced so many new opinions.

But what we most admire is the vast capacity of that intellect which, without effort, takes in at once all the domains of science—all the past, the present and the future, all the errors of two thousand years, all the encouraging signs of the passing times, all the bright hopes of the coming age.

He had a wonderful talent for packing thought close and rendering it portable.

His eloquence would alone have entitled him to a high rank in literature.

60

It is evident that he had each and every one of the mental gifts and each and every one of the acquirements that are so prodigally displayed in the Plays and Poems, and in much higher and richer degree than any other man of his time or of any previous time. He was a genius without a mate, a prodigy not matable. There was only one of him; the planet could not produce two of him at one birth, nor in one age. He could have written anything that is in the Plays and Poems. He could have written this:

The cloud-cap'd towers, the gorgeous palaces,

The solemn temples, the great globe itself,

Yea, all which it inherit, shall dissolve,

And, like an insubstantial pageant faded,

Leave not a rack behind. We are such stuff

As dreams are made on, and our little life

Is rounded with a sleep.

Also, he could have written this, but he refrained:

Good friend for Iesus sake forbeare

To digg the dust encloased heare:

Blest be ye man yt spares thes stones

And curst be ye yt moves my bones.

When a person reads the noble verses about the cloud-cap'd towers, he ought not to follow it immediately with Good friend for Iesus sake forbeare, because he will find the transition from great poetry to poor prose too violent for comfort. It will give him a shock. You never notice how commonplace and unpoetic gravel is, until you bite into a layer of it in a pie.

CHAPTER XI

Am I trying to convince anybody that Shakespeare did not write Shakespeare's Works? Ah, now, what do you take me for? Would I be so soft as that, after having known the human race familiarly for nearly seventy-four years? It would grieve me to know that any one could think so injuriously of me, so uncomplimentarily, so unadmiringly of me. No-no, I am aware that when even the brightest mind in our world has been trained up from childhood in a superstition of any kind, it will never be possible for that mind, in its maturity, to examine sincerely, dispassionately, and conscientiously any evidence or any circumstance which shall seem to cast a doubt upon the validity of that superstition. I doubt if I could do it myself. We always get at second hand our notions about systems of government; and high-tariff and low-tariff; and prohibition and anti-prohibition; and the holiness of peace and the glories of war; and codes of honor and codes of morals; and approval of the duel and disapproval of it; and our beliefs concerning the nature of cats; and our ideas as to whether the murder of helpless wild animals is base or is heroic; and our preferences in the matter of religious and political parties; and our acceptance or rejection of the Shakespeares and the Arthur Ortons and the Mrs. Eddys. We get them all at second-hand, we reason none of them out for ourselves. It is the way we are made. It is the way we are all made, and we can't help it, we can't change it. And whenever we have been furnished a fetish, and have been taught to believe in it, and love it and worship it, and refrain from examining it, there is no evidence, howsoever clear and strong, that can persuade us to withdraw from it our loyalty and our devotion. In morals, conduct, and beliefs we take the color of our environment and associations, and it is a color that can safely be warranted to wash. Whenever we have been furnished with a tar baby ostensibly stuffed with jewels, and warned that it will be dishonorable and irreverent to disembowel it and test the jewels, we keep our sacrilegious hands off it. We submit, not reluctantly, but rather gladly, for we are privately afraid we should find, upon examination, that the jewels are of the sort that are manufactured at North Adams, Mass.

I haven't any idea that Shakespeare will have to vacate his pedestal this side of the year 2209. Disbelief in him cannot come swiftly, disbelief in a healthy and deeply-loved tar baby has never been known to disintegrate swiftly, it is a very slow process. It took several thousand years to convince our fine race—including every splendid intellect in it—that there is no such thing as a witch; it has taken several thousand years to convince that same fine race—including every splendid intellect in it—that there is no such person as Satan; it has taken several centuries to remove perdition from the Protestant Church's program of postmortem entertainments; it has taken a weary long time to persuade American Presbyterians to give up infant damnation and try to bear it the best they can; and it looks as if their Scotch brethren will still be burning babies in the everlasting fires when Shakespeare comes down from his perch.

We are The Reasoning Race. We can't prove it by the above examples, and we can't prove it by the miraculous "histories" built by those Stratfordolaters out of a hatful of rags and a barrel of sawdust, but there is a plenty of other things we can prove it by, if I could think of them. We are The Reasoning Race, and when we find a vague file of chipmunk-tracks stringing through the dust of Stratford village, we know by our reasoning powers that Hercules has been along there. I feel that our fetish is safe for three centuries yet. The bust, too—there in the Stratford Church. The precious bust, the priceless bust, the calm bust, the serene bust, the emotionless bust, with the dandy moustache, and the putty face, unseamed of care—that face which has looked passionlessly down upon the awed pilgrim for a hundred and fifty years and will still look down upon the awed pilgrim three hundred more, with the deep, deep, deep, subtle, subtle, subtle, expression of a bladder.

CHAPTER XII—Irreverence

One of the most trying defects which I find in these—these—what shall I call them? for I will not apply injurious epithets to them, the way they do to us, such violations of courtesy being repugnant to my nature and my dignity. The furthest I can go in that direction is to call them by names of limited reverence—names merely descriptive, never unkind, never offensive, never tainted by harsh feeling. If *they* would do like this, they would feel better in their hearts. Very well, then—to proceed. One of the most trying defects which I find in these Stratfordolaters, these Shakesperoids, these thugs, these bangalores, these troglodytes, these herumfrodites, these blatherskites, these buccaneers, these bandoleers, is their spirit of irreverence. It is detectable in every utterance of theirs when they are talking about us. I am thankful that in me there is nothing of that spirit. When a thing is sacred to me it is impossible for me to be irreverent toward it. I cannot call to mind a single instance where I have ever been irreverent, except toward the things which were sacred to other people. Am I in the right? I think so. But I ask no one to take my unsupported word; no, look at the dictionary; let the dictionary decide. Here is the definition:

Irreverence. The quality or condition of irreverence toward God and sacred things.

What does the Hindu say? He says it is correct. He says irreverence is lack of respect for Vishnu, and Brahma, and Chrishna, and his other gods, and for his sacred cattle, and for his temples and the things within them. He endorses the definition, you see; and there are 300,000,000 Hindus or their equivalents back of him.

The dictionary had the acute idea that by using the capital G it could restrict irreverence to lack of reverence for *our* Deity and our sacred things, but that ingenious and rather sly idea miscarried: for by the simple process of spelling *his* deities with capitals the Hindu confiscates the definition and restricts it to his own sects, thus making it clearly compulsory upon us to revere *his* gods and *his* sacred things, and nobody's else. We can't say a word, for he has our own dictionary at his back, and its decision is final.

This law, reduced to its simplest terms, is this: 1. Whatever is sacred to the Christian must be held in reverence by everybody else; 2, whatever is sacred to the Hindu must be held in reverence by everybody else; 3, therefore, by consequence, logically, and indisputably, whatever is sacred to *me* must be held in reverence by everybody else.

Now then, what aggravates me is, that these troglodytes and muscovites and bandoleers and buccaneers are *also* trying to crowd in and share the benefit of the law, and compel everybody to revere their Shakespeare and hold him sacred. We can't have that: there's enough of us already. If you go on widening and spreading and inflating the privilege, it will presently come to be conceded that each man's sacred things are the *only* ones, and the rest of the human race will have to be humbly reverent toward them or suffer for it. That can surely happen, and when it happens, the word Irreverence will be regarded as the most meaningless, and foolish, and self-conceited, and insolent, and impudent and dictatorial word in the language. And people will say, "Whose business is it, what gods I worship and what things hold sacred? Who has the right to dictate to my conscience, and where did he get that right?"

We cannot afford to let that calamity come upon us. We must save the word from this destruction. There is but one way to do it, and that is, to stop the spread of the privilege, and strictly confine it to its present limits: that is, to all the Christian sects, to all the Hindu sects, and me. We do not need any more, the stock is watered enough, just as it is.

It would be better if the privilege were limited to me alone. I think so because I am the only sect that knows how to employ it gently, kindly, charitably, dispassionately. The other sects lack the quality of self-restraint. The Catholic Church says the most irreverent things about matters which are sacred to the Protestants, and the Protestant Church retorts in kind about the confessional and other matters which Catholics hold sacred; then both of these irreverencers turn upon Thomas Paine and charge *him* with irreverence. This is all unfortunate, because it makes it difficult for students equipped with only a low grade of mentality to find out what Irreverence really *is*.

It will surely be much better all around if the privilege of regulating the irreverent and keeping them in order shall eventually be withdrawn from all the sects but me. Then there will be no more quarrelling, no more bandying of disrespectful epithets, no more heart burnings.

There will then be nothing sacred involved in this Bacon-Shakespeare controversy except what is sacred to me. That will simplify the whole matter, and trouble will cease. There will be irreverence no longer, because I will not allow it. The first time those criminals charge me with irreverence for calling their Stratford myth an Arthur-Orton-Mary-Baker-Thompson-Eddy-Louis-the-Seventeenth-Veiled-Prophet-of-Khorassan will be the last. Taught by the methods found effective in extinguishing earlier offenders by the Inquisition, of holy memory, I shall know how to quiet them.

CHAPTER XIII

Isn't it odd, when you think of it: that you may list all the celebrated Englishmen, Irishmen, and Scotchmen of modern times, clear back to the first Tudors—a list containing five hundred names, shall we say?—and you can go to the histories, biographies and cyclopedias and learn the particulars of the lives of every one of them. Every one of them except one—the most famous, the most renowned—by far the most illustrious of them all—Shakespeare! You can get the details of the lives of all the celebrated ecclesiastics in the list; all the celebrated tragedians, comedians, singers, dancers, orators, judges, lawyers, poets, dramatists, historians, biographers, editors, inventors, reformers, statesmen, generals, admirals, discoverers, prize-fighters, murderers, pirates, conspirators, horse-jockeys, bunco-steerers, misers, swindlers, explorers, adventurers by land and sea, bankers, financiers, astronomers, naturalists, Claimants, impostors, chemists, biologists, geologists, philologists, college presidents and professors, architects, engineers, painters, sculptors, politicians, agitators, rebels, revolutionists, patriots, demagogues, clowns, cooks, freaks, philosophers, burglars, highwaymen, journalists, physicians, surgeons— you can get the life-histories of all of them but *one*. Just one—the most extraordinary and the most celebrated of them all—Shakespeare!

You may add to the list the thousand celebrated persons furnished by the rest of Christendom in the past four centuries, and you can find out the life-histories of all those people, too. You will then have listed 1500 celebrities, and you can trace the authentic life-histories of the whole of them. Save one—far and away the most colossal prodigy of the entire accumulation— Shakespeare! About him you can find out *nothing*. Nothing of even the slightest importance. Nothing worth the trouble of stowing away in your memory. Nothing that even remotely indicates that he was ever anything more than a distinctly common-place person—a manager, an actor of inferior grade, a small trader in a small village that did not regard him as a person of any consequence, and had forgotten all about him before he was fairly cold in his grave. We can go to the records and find out the life-history of every renowned *race-horse* of modern times—but not Shakespeare's! There are many reasons why, and they have been furnished in cartloads (of guess and conjecture) by those troglodytes; but there is one that is worth all the rest of the reasons put together, and is abundantly sufficient all by itself—*he hadn't any history to record.* There is no way of getting around that deadly fact. And no sane way has yet been discovered of getting around its formidable significance.

Its quite plain significance—to any but those thugs (I do not use the term unkindly) is, that Shakespeare had no prominence while he lived, and none until he had been dead two or three generations. The Plays enjoyed high fame from the beginning; and if he wrote them it seems a pity the world did not find it out. He ought to have explained that he was the author, and not merely a *nom de plume* for another man to hide behind. If he had been less intemperately solicitous about his bones, and more solicitous about his Works, it would have been better for his good name, and a kindness to us. The bones were not important. They will moulder away, they will turn to dust, but the Works will endure until the last sun goes down.

MARK TWAIN.

P.S. *March* 25. About two months ago I was illuminating this Autobiography with some notions of mine concerning the Bacon-Shakespeare controversy, and I then took occasion to air the opinion that the Stratford Shakespeare was a person of no public consequence or celebrity during his lifetime, but was utterly obscure and unimportant. And not only in great London, but also in the little village where he was born, where he lived a quarter of a century, and where he died and was buried. I argued that if he had been a person of any note at all, aged villagers would have had much to tell about him many and many a year after his death, instead of being unable to furnish inquirers a single fact connected with him. I believed, and I still believe, that if he had been famous, his notoriety would have lasted as long as mine has lasted in my native village out in Missouri. It is a good argument, a prodigiously strong one, and a most formidable one for even the most gifted, and ingenious, and plausible Stratfordolater to get around or explain away. To-day a Hannibal *Courier-Post* of recent date has reached me, with an article in it which reinforces my contention that a really celebrated person cannot be forgotten in his village in the short space of sixty years. I will make an extract from it:

Hannibal, as a city, may have many sins to answer for, but ingratitude is not one of them, or reverence for the great men she has produced, and as the years go by her greatest son Mark Twain, or S. L. Clemens as a few of the unlettered call him, grows in the estimation and regard of the residents of the town he made famous and the town that made him famous. His name is associated with every old building that is torn down to make way for the modern structures demanded by a rapidly growing city, and with every hill or cave over or through which he might by any possibility have roamed, while the many points of interest which he wove into his stories, such as Holiday Hill, Jackson's Island, or Mark Twain Cave, are now monuments to his genius. Hannibal is glad of any opportunity to do him honor as he has honored her.

So it has happened that the "old timers" who went to school with Mark or were with him on some of his usual escapades have been honored with large audiences whenever they were in a reminiscent mood and condescended to tell of their intimacy with the ordinary boy who came to be a very extraordinary humorist and whose every boyish act is now seen to have been indicative of what was to come. Like Aunt Beckey and Mrs. Clemens, they can now see that Mark was hardly appreciated when he lived here and that the things he did as a boy and was whipped for doing were not all bad after all. So they have been in no hesitancy about drawing out the bad things he did as well as the good in their efforts to get a "Mark Twain story," all incidents being viewed in the light of his present fame, until the volume of "Twainiana" is already considerable and growing in proportion as the "old timers" drop away and the stories are retold second and third hand by their descendants. With some seventy-three years young and living in a villa instead of a house he is a fair target, and let him incorporate, copyright, or patent himself as he will, there are some of his "works" that will go swooping up Hannibal chimneys as long as gray-beards gather about the fires and begin with "I've heard father tell" or possibly "Once when I."

The Mrs. Clemens referred to is my mother—*was* my mother.

And here is another extract from a Hannibal paper. Of date twenty days ago:

Miss Becca Blankenship died at the home of William Dickason, 408 Rock Street, at 2.30 o'clock yesterday afternoon, aged 72 years. The deceased was a sister of "Huckleberry Finn," one of the famous characters in Mark Twain's *Tom Sawyer*. She had been a member of the Dickason family—the housekeeper—for nearly forty-five years, and was a highly respected lady. For the past eight years she had been an invalid, but was as well cared for by Mr. Dickason and his family as if she had been a near relative. She was a member of the Park Methodist Church and a Christian woman.

I remember her well. I have a picture of her in my mind which was graven there, clear and sharp and vivid, sixty-three years ago. She was at that time nine years old, and I was about eleven. I remember where she stood, and how she looked; and I can still see her bare feet, her bare head, her brown face, and her short tow-linen frock. She was crying. What it was about, I have long ago forgotten. But it was the tears that preserved the picture for me, no doubt. She was a good child, I can say that for her. She knew me nearly seventy years ago. Did she forget me, in the course of time? I think not. If she had lived in Stratford in Shakespeare's time, would she have forgotten him? Yes. For he was never famous during his lifetime, he was utterly obscure in Stratford, and there wouldn't be any occasion to remember him after he had been dead a week.

"Injun Joe," "Jimmy Finn," and "General Gaines" were prominent and very intemperate ne'er-do-weels in Hannibal two generations ago. Plenty of gray-heads there remember them to this day, and can tell you about them. Isn't it curious that two "town-drunkards" and one half-breed loafer should leave behind them, in a remote Missourian village, a fame a hundred times greater and several hundred times more particularized in the matter of definite facts than Shakespeare left behind him in the village where he had lived the half of his lifetime?

MARK TWAIN.

Footnotes:

[1] Four fathoms—twenty-four feet.

[2] From chapter XIII of "The Shakespeare Problem Restated."

About Author

Samuel Langhorne Clemens (November 30, 1835 – April 21, 1910), known by his pen name **Mark Twain**, was an American writer, humorist, entrepreneur, publisher, and lecturer. He was lauded as the "greatest humorist [the United States] has produced", and William Faulkner called him "the father of American literature". His novels include The Adventures of Tom Sawyer (1876) and its sequel, the Adventures of Huckleberry Finn (1884),the latter often called "The Great American Novel".

Twain was raised in Hannibal, Missouri, which later provided the setting for Tom Sawyer and Huckleberry Finn. He served an apprenticeship with a printer and then worked as a typesetter, contributing articles to the newspaper of his older brother Orion Clemens. He later became a riverboat pilot on the Mississippi River before heading west to join Orion in Nevada. He referred humorously to his lack of success at mining, turning to journalism for the Virginia City Territorial Enterprise. His humorous story, "The Celebrated Jumping Frog of Calaveras County", was published in 1865, based on a story that he heard at Angels Hotel in Angels Camp, California, where he had spent some time as a miner. The short story brought international attention and was even translated into French. His wit and satire, in prose and in speech, earned praise from critics and peers, and he was a friend to presidents, artists, industrialists, and European royalty.

Twain earned a great deal of money from his writings and lectures, but he invested in ventures that lost most of it—such as the Paige Compositor, a mechanical typesetter that failed because of its complexity and imprecision. He filed for bankruptcy in the wake of these financial setbacks, but he eventually overcame his financial troubles with the help of Henry Huttleston Rogers. He eventually paid all his creditors in full, even though his bankruptcy relieved him of having to do so. Twain was born shortly after an appearance of Halley's Comet, and he predicted that he would "go out with it" as well; he died the day after the comet returned.

Biography

Early life

Samuel Langhorne Clemens was born on November 30, 1835, in Florida, Missouri, the sixth of seven children born to Jane (née Lampton; 1803–1890), a native of Kentucky, and John Marshall Clemens (1798–1847), a native of Virginia. His parents met when his father moved to Missouri, and they were married in 1823. Twain was of Cornish, English, and Scots-Irish descent. Only three of his siblings survived childhood: Orion (1825–1897), Henry (1838–1858), and Pamela (1827–1904). His sister Margaret (1830–1839) died when Twain was three, and his brother Benjamin (1832–1842) died three years later. His brother Pleasant Hannibal (1828) died at three weeks of age.

When he was four, Twain's family moved to Hannibal, Missouri,a port town on the Mississippi River that inspired the fictional town of St. Petersburg in The Adventures of Tom Sawyer and the Adventures of Huckleberry Finn. Slavery was legal in Missouri at the time, and it became a theme in these writings. His father was an attorney and judge, who died of pneumonia in 1847, when Twain was 11. The next year, Twain left school after the fifth grade to become a printer's apprentice. In 1851, he began working as a typesetter, contributing articles and humorous sketches to the Hannibal Journal, a newspaper that Orion owned. When he was 18, he left Hannibal and worked as a printer in New York City, Philadelphia, St. Louis, and Cincinnati, joining the newly formed International Typographical Union, the printers trade union. He educated himself in public libraries in the evenings, finding wider information than at a conventional school.

Twain describes his boyhood in Life on the Mississippi, stating that "there was but one permanent ambition" among his comrades: to be a steamboatman.

> Pilot was the grandest position of all. The pilot, even in those days of trivial wages, had a princely salary – from a hundred and fifty to two hundred and fifty dollars a month, and no board to pay.

As Twain describes it, the pilot's prestige exceeded that of the captain. The pilot had to:

...get up a warm personal acquaintanceship with every old snag and one-limbed cottonwood and every obscure wood pile that ornaments the banks of this river for twelve hundred miles; and more than that, must... actually know where these things are in the dark

Steamboat pilot Horace E. Bixby took Twain on as a cub pilot to teach him the river between New Orleans and St. Louis for $500 (equivalent to $15,000 in 2019), payable out of Twain's first wages after graduating. Twain studied the Mississippi, learning its landmarks, how to navigate its currents effectively, and how to read the river and its constantly shifting channels, reefs, submerged snags, and rocks that would "tear the life out of the strongest vessel that ever floated". It was more than two years before he received his pilot's license. Piloting also gave him his pen name from "mark twain", the leadsman's cry for a measured river depth of two fathoms (12 feet), which was safe water for a steamboat.

As a young pilot, Clemens served on the steamer A. B. Chambers with Grant Marsh, who became famous for his exploits as a steamboat captain on the Missouri River. The two liked each other, and admired one another, and maintained a correspondence for many years after Clemens left the river.

While training, Samuel convinced his younger brother Henry to work with him, and even arranged a post of mud clerk for him on the steamboat Pennsylvania. On June 13, 1858, the steamboat's boiler exploded; Henry succumbed to his wounds on June 21. Twain claimed to have foreseen this death in a dream a month earlier,:275 which inspired his interest in parapsychology; he was an early member of the Society for Psychical Research Twain was guilt-stricken and held himself responsible for the rest of his life. He continued to work on the river and was a river pilot until the Civil War broke out in 1861, when traffic was curtailed along the Mississippi River. At the start of hostilities, he enlisted briefly in a local Confederate unit. He later wrote the sketch "The Private History of a Campaign That Failed", describing how he and his friends had been Confederate volunteers for two weeks before disbanding.

He then left for Nevada to work for his brother Orion, who was Secretary of the Nevada Territory. Twain describes the episode in his book Roughing It.

Travels

Orion became secretary to Nevada Territory governor James W. Nye in 1861, and Twain joined him when he moved west. The brothers traveled more than two weeks on a stagecoach across the Great Plains and the Rocky Mountains, visiting the Mormon community in Salt Lake City.

Twain's journey ended in the silver-mining town of Virginia City, Nevada, where he became a miner on the Comstock Lode. He failed as a miner and went to work at the Virginia City newspaper Territorial Enterprise, working under a friend, the writer Dan DeQuille. He first used his pen name here on February 3, 1863, when he wrote a humorous travel account entitled "Letter From Carson – re: Joe Goodman; party at Gov. Johnson's; music" and signed it "Mark Twain".

His experiences in the American West inspired Roughing It, written during 1870–71 and published in 1872. His experiences in Angels Camp (in Calaveras County, California) provided material for "The Celebrated Jumping Frog of Calaveras County" (1865).

Twain moved to San Francisco in 1864, still as a journalist, and met writers such as Bret Harte and Artemus Ward. He may have been romantically involved with the poet Ina Coolbrith.

His first success as a writer came when his humorous tall tale "The Celebrated Jumping Frog of Calaveras County" was published on November 18, 1865, in the New York weekly The Saturday Press, bringing him national attention. A year later, he traveled to the Sandwich Islands (present-day Hawaii) as a reporter for the Sacramento Union. His letters to the Union were popular and became the basis for his first lectures.

In 1867, a local newspaper funded his trip to the Mediterranean aboard the Quaker City, including a tour of Europe and the Middle East. He wrote a collection of travel letters which were later compiled as The Innocents Abroad (1869). It was on this trip that he met fellow passenger Charles Langdon, who showed him a picture of his sister Olivia. Twain later claimed to have fallen in love at first sight.

Upon returning to the United States, Twain was offered honorary membership in Yale University's secret society Scroll and Key in 1868. Its devotion to "fellowship, moral and literary self-improvement, and charity" suited him well.

Marriage and children

Twain and Olivia Langdon corresponded throughout 1868. She rejected his first marriage proposal, but they were married in Elmira, New York in February 1870, where he courted her and managed to overcome her father's initial reluctance. She came from a "wealthy but liberal family"; through her, he met abolitionists, "socialists, principled atheists and activists for women's rights and social equality", including Harriet Beecher Stowe (his next-door neighbor in Hartford, Connecticut), Frederick Douglass, and writer and utopian socialist William Dean Howells, who became a long-time friend. The couple lived in Buffalo, New York, from 1869 to 1871. He owned a stake in the Buffalo Express newspaper and worked as an editor and writer. While they were living in Buffalo, their son Langdon died of diphtheria at the age of 19 months. They had three daughters: Susy (1872–1896), Clara (1874–1962), and Jean (1880–1909).

Twain moved his family to Hartford, Connecticut, where he arranged the building of a home starting in 1873. In the 1870s and 1880s, the family summered at Quarry Farm in Elmira, the home of Olivia's sister, Susan Crane. In 1874, Susan had a study built apart from the main house so that Twain would have a quiet place in which to write. Also, he smoked cigars constantly, and Susan did not want him to do so in her house.

Twain wrote many of his classic novels during his 17 years in Hartford (1874–1891) and over 20 summers at Quarry Farm. They include The Adventures of Tom Sawyer (1876), The Prince and the Pauper (1881), Life on the Mississippi (1883), Adventures of Huckleberry Finn (1884), and A Connecticut Yankee in King Arthur's Court (1889).

The couple's marriage lasted 34 years until Olivia's death in 1904. All of the Clemens family are buried in Elmira's Woodlawn Cemetery.

Love of science and technology

Twain was fascinated with science and scientific inquiry. He developed a close and lasting friendship with Nikola Tesla, and the two spent much time together in Tesla's laboratory.

Twain patented three inventions, including an "Improvement in Adjustable and Detachable Straps for Garments" (to replace suspenders) and a history trivia game. Most commercially successful was a self-pasting scrapbook; a dried adhesive on the pages needed only to be moistened before use. Over 25,000 were sold.

Twain was an early proponent of fingerprinting as a forensic technique, featuring it in a tall tale in Life on the Mississippi (1883) and as a central plot element in the novel Pudd'nhead Wilson (1894).

Twain's novel A Connecticut Yankee in King Arthur's Court (1889) features a time traveler from the contemporary U.S., using his knowledge of science to introduce modern technology to Arthurian England. This type of historical manipulation became a trope of speculative fiction as alternate histories.

In 1909, Thomas Edison visited Twain at his home in Redding, Connecticut and filmed him. Part of the footage was used in The Prince and the Pauper (1909), a two-reel short film. It is the only known existing film footage of Twain.

Financial troubles

Twain made a substantial amount of money through his writing, but he lost a great deal through investments. He invested mostly in new inventions and technology, particularly the Paige typesetting machine. It was a beautifully engineered mechanical marvel that amazed viewers when it worked, but it was prone to breakdowns. Twain spent $300,000 (equal to $9,000,000 in inflation-adjusted terms) on it between 1880 and 1894, but before it could be perfected it was rendered obsolete by the Linotype. He lost the bulk of his book profits, as well as a substantial portion of his wife's inheritance.

Twain also lost money through his publishing house, Charles L. Webster and Company, which enjoyed initial success selling the memoirs of Ulysses S. Grant but failed soon afterward, losing money on a biography of Pope Leo XIII. Fewer than 200 copies were sold.

Twain and his family closed down their expensive Hartford home in response to the dwindling income and moved to Europe in June 1891. William M. Laffan of The New York Sun and the McClure Newspaper Syndicate offered him the publication of a series of six European letters. Twain, Olivia, and their daughter Susy were all faced with health problems, and they believed that it would be of benefit to visit European baths.:175 The family stayed mainly in France, Germany, and Italy until May 1895, with longer spells at Berlin (winter 1891/92), Florence (fall and winter 1892/93), and Paris (winters and springs 1893/94 and 1894/95). During that period, Twain returned four times to New York due to his enduring business troubles. He took "a cheap room" in September 1893 at $1.50 per day (equivalent to $43 in 2019) at The Players Club, which he had to keep until March 1894; meanwhile, he became "the Belle of New York," in the words of biographer Albert Bigelow Paine.

Twain's writings and lectures enabled him to recover financially, combined with the help of his friend, Henry Huttleston Rogers. He began a friendship with the financier in 1893, a principal of Standard Oil, that lasted the remainder of his life. Rogers first made him file for bankruptcy in April 1894, then had him transfer the copyrights on his written works to his wife to prevent creditors from gaining possession of them. Finally, Rogers took absolute charge of Twain's money until all his creditors were paid.

Twain accepted an offer from Robert Sparrow Smythe and embarked on a year-long, around the world lecture tour in July 1895 to pay off his creditors in full, although he was no longer under any legal obligation to do so. It was a long, arduous journey and he was sick much of the time, mostly from a cold and a carbuncle. The first part of the itinerary took him across northern America to British Columbia, Canada, until the second half of August. For the second part, he sailed across the Pacific Ocean. His scheduled lecture in Honolulu, Hawaii had to be canceled due to a cholera epidemic.[188] Twain went on to Fiji, Australia, New Zealand, Sri Lanka, India, Mauritius, and South Africa. His three months in India became the centerpiece of his 712-page book Following the Equator. In the second half of July 1896, he sailed back to England, completing his circumnavigation of the world begun 14 months before.

Twain and his family spent four more years in Europe, mainly in England and Austria (October 1897 to May 1899), with longer spells in London and Vienna. Clara had wished to study the piano under Theodor Leschetizky in Vienna.:192–211 However, Jean's health did not benefit from consulting with specialists in Vienna, the "City of Doctors". The family moved to London in spring 1899, following a lead by Poultney Bigelow who had a good experience being treated by Dr. Jonas Henrik Kellgren, a Swedish osteopathic practitioner in Belgravia. They were persuaded to spend the summer at Kellgren's sanatorium by the lake in the Swedish village of Sanna. Coming back in fall, they continued the treatment in London, until Twain was convinced by lengthy inquiries in America that similar osteopathic expertise was available there.

In mid-1900, he was the guest of newspaper proprietor Hugh Gilzean-Reid at Dollis Hill House, located on the north side of London. Twain wrote that he had "never seen any place that was so satisfactorily situated, with its noble trees and stretch of country, and everything that went to make life delightful, and all within a biscuit's throw of the metropolis of the world."He then returned to America in October 1900, having earned enough to pay off his debts. In winter 1900/01, he became his country's most prominent opponent of imperialism, raising the issue in his speeches, interviews, and writings. In January 1901, he began serving as vice-president of the Anti-Imperialist League of New York.

Speaking engagements

Twain was in great demand as a featured speaker, performing solo humorous talks similar to modern stand-up comedy. He gave paid talks to many men's clubs, including the Authors' Club, Beefsteak Club, Vagabonds, White Friars, and Monday Evening Club of Hartford.

In the late 1890s, he spoke to the Savage Club in London and was elected an honorary member. He was told that only three men had been so honored, including the Prince of Wales, and he replied: "Well, it must make the Prince feel mighty fine.":197 He visited Melbourne and Sydney in 1895 as part of a world lecture tour. In 1897, he spoke to the Concordia Press Club in Vienna as a special guest, following the diplomat Charlemagne Tower, Jr. He delivered the speech "Die Schrecken der Deutschen Sprache" ("The Horrors of the German Language")—in German—to the great amusement of the audience.:50 In 1901, he was invited to speak at Princeton University's Cliosophic Literary Society, where he was made an honorary member.

Canadian visits

In 1881, Twain was honored at a banquet in Montreal, Canada where he made reference to securing a copyright. In 1883, he paid a brief visit to Ottawa, and he visited Toronto twice in 1884 and 1885 on a reading tour with George Washington Cable, known as the "Twins of Genius" tour.

The reason for the Toronto visits was to secure Canadian and British copyrights for his upcoming book Adventures of Huckleberry Finn,to which he had alluded in his Montreal visit. The reason for the Ottawa visit had been to secure Canadian and British copyrights for Life on the Mississippi Publishers in Toronto had printed unauthorized editions of his books at the time, before an international copyright agreement was established in 1891. These were sold in the United States as well as in Canada, depriving him of royalties. He estimated that Belford Brothers' edition of The Adventures of Tom Sawyer alone had cost him ten thousand dollars (equivalent to $280,000 in 2019). He had unsuccessfully attempted to secure the rights for The Prince and the Pauper in 1881, in conjunction with his Montreal trip. Eventually, he received legal advice to register a copyright in Canada (for both Canada and Britain) prior to publishing in the United States, which would restrain the Canadian publishers from printing a version when the American edition was published. There was a requirement that a copyright be registered to a Canadian resident; he addressed this by his short visits to the country.

Later life and death

Twain lived in his later years at 14 West 10th Street in Manhattan. He passed through a period of deep depression which began in 1896 when his daughter Susy died of meningitis. Olivia's death in 1904 and Jean's on December 24, 1909, deepened his gloom. On May 20, 1909, his close friend Henry Rogers died suddenly. In April 1906, he heard that his friend Ina Coolbrith had lost nearly all that she owned in the 1906 San Francisco earthquake, and he volunteered a few autographed portrait photographs to be sold for her benefit. To further aid Coolbrith, George Wharton James visited Twain in New York and arranged for a new portrait session. He was resistant initially, but he eventually admitted that four of the resulting images were the finest ones ever taken of him. In September, Twain started publishing chapters from his autobiography in the North American Review. The same year, Charlotte Teller, a writer living with her grandmother at 3 Fifth Avenue, began an acquaintanceship with him which "lasted several years and may have included romantic intentions" on his part.

Twain formed a club in 1906 for girls whom he viewed as surrogate granddaughters called the Angel Fish and Aquarium Club. The dozen or so members ranged in age from 10 to 16. He exchanged letters with his "Angel Fish" girls and invited them to concerts and the theatre and to play games. Twain wrote in 1908 that the club was his "life's chief delight". In 1907, he met Dorothy Quick (aged 11) on a transatlantic crossing, beginning "a friendship that was to last until the very day of his death".

Oxford University awarded Twain an honorary doctorate in letters in 1907.

Twain was born two weeks after Halley's Comet's closest approach in 1835; he said in 1909:

84

I came in with Halley's Comet in 1835. It is coming again next year, and I expect to go out with it. It will be the greatest disappointment of my life if I don't go out with Halley's Comet. The Almighty has said, no doubt: "Now here are these two unaccountable freaks; they came in together, they must go out together".

Twain's prediction was accurate; he died of a heart attack on April 21, 1910, in Redding, Connecticut, one day after the comet's closest approach to Earth.

Upon hearing of Twain's death, President William Howard Taft said:

Mark Twain gave pleasure – real intellectual enjoyment – to millions, and his works will continue to give such pleasure to millions yet to come … His humor was American, but he was nearly as much appreciated by Englishmen and people of other countries as by his own countrymen. He has made an enduring part of American literature.

Twain's funeral was at the Brick Presbyterian Church on Fifth Avenue, New York. He is buried in his wife's family plot at Woodlawn Cemetery in Elmira, New York. The Langdon family plot is marked by a 12-foot monument (two fathoms, or "mark twain") placed there by his surviving daughter Clara. There is also a smaller headstone. He expressed a preference for cremation (for example, in Life on the Mississippi), but he acknowledged that his surviving family would have the last word.

Officials in Connecticut and New York estimated the value of Twain's estate at $471,000 ($13,000,000 today).

Writing

Overview

Twain began his career writing light, humorous verse, but he became a chronicler of the vanities, hypocrisies, and murderous acts of mankind. At mid-career, he combined rich humor, sturdy narrative, and social criticism in Huckleberry Finn. He was a master of rendering colloquial speech and helped to create and popularize a distinctive American literature built on American themes and language.

Many of his works have been suppressed at times for various reasons. The Adventures of Huckleberry Finn has been repeatedly restricted in American high schools, not least for its frequent use of the word "nigger", which was in common usage in the pre-Civil War period in which the novel was set.

A complete bibliography of Twain's works is nearly impossible to compile because of the vast number of pieces he wrote (often in obscure newspapers) and his use of several different pen names. Additionally, a large portion of his speeches and lectures have been lost or were not recorded; thus, the compilation of Twain's works is an ongoing process. Researchers rediscovered published material as recently as 1995 and 2015.

Early journalism and travelogues

Twain was writing for the Virginia City newspaper the Territorial Enterprise in 1863 when he met lawyer Tom Fitch, editor of the competing newspaper Virginia Daily Union and known as the "silver-tongued orator of the Pacific".:51 He credited Fitch with giving him his "first really profitable lesson" in writing. "When I first began to lecture, and in my earlier writings," Twain later commented, "my sole idea was to make comic capital out of everything I saw and heard." In 1866, he presented his lecture on the Sandwich Islands to a crowd in Washoe City, Nevada. Afterwards, Fitch told him:

> Clemens, your lecture was magnificent. It was eloquent, moving, sincere. Never in my entire life have I listened to such a magnificent piece of descriptive narration. But you committed one unpardonable sin – the unpardonable sin. It is a sin you must never commit again. You closed a most eloquent description, by which you had keyed your audience up to a pitch of the intensest interest, with a piece of atrocious anti-climax which nullified all the really fine effect you had produced.

It was in these days that Twain became a writer of the Sagebrush School; he was known later as its most famous member. His first important work was "The Celebrated Jumping Frog of Calaveras County," published in the New York Saturday Press on November 18, 1865. After a burst of popularity, the Sacramento Union commissioned him to write letters about his travel experiences. The first journey that he took for this job was to ride the steamer Ajax on its maiden voyage to the Sandwich Islands (Hawaii). All the while, he was writing letters to the newspaper that were meant for publishing, chronicling his experiences with humor. These letters proved to be the genesis to his work with the San Francisco Alta California newspaper, which designated him a traveling correspondent for a trip from San Francisco to New York City via the Panama isthmus.

On June 8, 1867, he set sail on the pleasure cruiser Quaker City for five months, and this trip resulted in The Innocents Abroad or The New Pilgrims' Progress. In 1872, he published his second piece of travel literature, Roughing It, as an account of his journey from Missouri to Nevada, his subsequent life in the American West, and his visit to Hawaii. The book lampoons American and Western society in the same way that Innocents critiqued the various countries of Europe and the Middle East. His next work was The Gilded Age: A Tale of Today, his first attempt at writing a novel. The book, written with his neighbor Charles Dudley Warner, is also his only collaboration.

Twain's next work drew on his experiences on the Mississippi River. Old Times on the Mississippi was a series of sketches published in the Atlantic Monthly in 1875 featuring his disillusionment with Romanticism. Old Times eventually became the starting point for Life on the Mississippi.

Tom Sawyer and Huckleberry Finn

Twain's next major publication was The Adventures of Tom Sawyer, which draws on his youth in Hannibal. Tom Sawyer was modeled on Twain as a child, with traces of schoolmates John Briggs and Will Bowen. The book also introduces Huckleberry Finn in a supporting role, based on Twain's boyhood friend Tom Blankenship.

The Prince and the Pauper was not as well received, despite a storyline that is common in film and literature today. The book tells the story of two boys born on the same day who are physically identical, acting as a social commentary as the prince and pauper switch places. Twain had started Adventures of Huckleberry Finn (which he consistently had problems completing) and had completed his travel book A Tramp Abroad, which describes his travels through central and southern Europe.

Twain's next major published work was the Adventures of Huckleberry Finn, which confirmed him as a noteworthy American writer. Some have called it the first Great American Novel, and the book has become required reading in many schools throughout the United States. Huckleberry Finn was an offshoot from Tom Sawyer and had a more serious tone than its predecessor. Four hundred manuscript pages were written in mid-1876, right after the publication of Tom Sawyer. The last fifth of Huckleberry Finn is subject to much controversy. Some say that Twain experienced a "failure of nerve," as critic Leo Marx puts it. Ernest Hemingway once said of Huckleberry Finn:

> If you read it, you must stop where the Nigger Jim is stolen from the boys. That is the real end. The rest is just cheating.

Hemingway also wrote in the same essay:

> All modern American literature comes from one book by Mark Twain called Huckleberry Finn.

Near the completion of Huckleberry Finn, Twain wrote Life on the Mississippi, which is said to have heavily influenced the novel. The travel work recounts Twain's memories and new experiences after a 22-year absence from the Mississippi River. In it, he also explains that "Mark Twain" was the call made when the boat was in safe water, indicating a depth of two fathoms (12 feet or 3.7 metres).

Later writing

Twain produced President Ulysses S. Grant's Memoirs through his fledgling publishing house, Charles L. Webster & Company, which he co-owned with Charles L. Webster, his nephew by marriage.

At this time he also wrote "The Private History of a Campaign That Failed" for The Century Magazine. This piece detailed his two-week stint in a Confederate militia during the Civil War. He next focused on A Connecticut Yankee in King Arthur's Court, written with the same historical fiction style as The Prince and the Pauper. A Connecticut Yankee showed the absurdities of political and social norms by setting them in the court of King Arthur. The book was started in December 1885, then shelved a few months later until the summer of 1887, and eventually finished in the spring of 1889.

His next large-scale work was Pudd'nhead Wilson, which he wrote rapidly, as he was desperately trying to stave off bankruptcy. From November 12 to December 14, 1893, Twain wrote 60,000 words for the novel. Critics[who?] have pointed to this rushed completion as the cause of the novel's rough organization and constant disruption of the plot. This novel also contains the tale of two boys born on the same day who switch positions in life, like The Prince and the Pauper. It was first published serially in Century Magazine and, when it was finally published in book form, Pudd'nhead Wilson appeared as the main title; however, the "subtitles" make the entire title read: The Tragedy of Pudd'nhead Wilson and the Comedy of The Extraordinary Twins.

Twain's next venture was a work of straight fiction that he called Personal Recollections of Joan of Arc and dedicated to his wife. He had long said[where?] that this was the work that he was most proud of, despite the criticism that he received for it. The book had been a dream of his since childhood, and he claimed that he had found a manuscript detailing the life of Joan of Arc when he was an adolescent. This was another piece that he was convinced would save his publishing company. His financial adviser Henry Huttleston Rogers quashed that idea and got Twain out of that business altogether, but the book was published nonetheless.

To pay the bills and keep his business projects afloat, Twain had begun to write articles and commentary furiously, with diminishing returns, but it was not enough. He filed for bankruptcy in 1894. During this time of dire financial straits, he published several literary reviews in newspapers to help make ends meet. He famously derided James Fenimore Cooper in his article detailing Cooper's "Literary Offenses". He became an extremely outspoken critic of other authors and other critics; he suggested that, before praising Cooper's work, Thomas Lounsbury, Brander Matthews, and Wilkie Collins "ought to have read some of it".

George Eliot, Jane Austen, and Robert Louis Stevenson also fell under Twain's attack during this time period, beginning around 1890 and continuing until his death. He outlines what he considers to be "quality writing" in several letters and essays, in addition to providing a source for the "tooth and claw" style of literary criticism. He places emphasis on concision, utility of word choice, and realism; he complains, for example, that Cooper's Deerslayer purports to be realistic but has several shortcomings. Ironically, several of his own works were later criticized for lack of continuity (Adventures of Huckleberry Finn) and organization (Pudd'nhead Wilson).

Twain's wife died in 1904 while the couple were staying at the Villa di Quarto in Florence. After some time had passed he published some works that his wife, his de facto editor and censor throughout her married life, had looked down upon. The Mysterious Stranger is perhaps the best known, depicting various visits of Satan to earth. This particular work was not published in Twain's lifetime. His manuscripts included three versions, written between 1897 and 1905: the so-called Hannibal, Eseldorf, and Print Shop versions. The resulting confusion led to extensive publication of a jumbled version, and only recently have the original versions become available as Twain wrote them.

Twain's last work was his autobiography, which he dictated and thought would be most entertaining if he went off on whims and tangents in non-chronological order. Some archivists and compilers have rearranged the biography into a more conventional form, thereby eliminating some of Twain's humor and the flow of the book. The first volume of the autobiography, over 736 pages, was published by the University of California in November 2010, 100 years after his death, as Twain wished. It soon became an unexpected best-seller, making Twain one of a very few authors publishing new best-selling volumes in the 19th, 20th, and 21st centuries.

Censorship

Twain's works have been subjected to censorship efforts. According to Stuart (2013), "Leading these banning campaigns, generally, were religious organizations or individuals in positions of influence – not so much working librarians, who had been instilled with that American "library spirit" which honored intellectual freedom (within bounds of course)". In 1905, the Brooklyn Public Library banned both The Adventures of Huckleberry Finn and The Adventures of Tom Sawyer from the children's department because of their language.

Views

Twain's views became more radical as he grew older. In a letter to friend and fellow writer William Dean Howells in 1887 he acknowledged that his views had changed and developed over his lifetime, referring to one of his favorite works:

> When I finished Carlyle's French Revolution in 1871, I was a Girondin; every time I have read it since, I have read it differently – being influenced and changed, little by little, by life and environment ... and now I lay the book down once more, and recognize that I am a Sansculotte! And not a pale, characterless Sansculotte, but a Marat.

Anti-imperialist

Before 1899, Twain was an ardent imperialist. In the late 1860s and early 1870s, he spoke out strongly in favor of American interests in the Hawaiian Islands. He said the war with Spain in 1898 was "the worthiest" war ever fought. In 1899, however, he reversed course. In the New York Herald, October 16, 1900, Twain describes his transformation and political awakening, in the context of the Philippine–American War, to anti-imperialism:

> I wanted the American eagle to go screaming into the Pacific ... Why not spread its wings over the Philippines, I asked myself? ... I said to myself, Here are a people who have suffered for three centuries. We can make them as free as ourselves, give them a government and country of their own, put a miniature of the American Constitution afloat in the Pacific, start a brand new republic to take its place among the free nations of the world. It seemed to me a great task to which we had addressed ourselves.

> But I have thought some more, since then, and I have read carefully the treaty of Paris [which ended the Spanish–American War], and I have seen that we do not intend to free, but to subjugate the people of the Philippines. We have gone there to conquer, not to redeem.

> It should, it seems to me, be our pleasure and duty to make those people free, and let them deal with their own domestic questions in

their own way. And so I am an anti-imperialist. I am opposed to having the eagle put its talons on any other land.

During the Boxer rebellion, Twain said that "the Boxer is a patriot. He loves his country better than he does the countries of other people. I wish him success."

From 1901, soon after his return from Europe, until his death in 1910, Twain was vice-president of the American Anti-Imperialist League, which opposed the annexation of the Philippines by the United States and had "tens of thousands of members". He wrote many political pamphlets for the organization. The Incident in the Philippines, posthumously published in 1924, was in response to the Moro Crater Massacre, in which six hundred Moros were killed. Many of his neglected and previously uncollected writings on anti-imperialism appeared for the first time in book form in 1992.

Twain was critical of imperialism in other countries as well. In Following the Equator, Twain expresses "hatred and condemnation of imperialism of all stripes". He was highly critical of European imperialists, such as Cecil Rhodes, who greatly expanded the British Empire, and Leopold II, King of the Belgians. King Leopold's Soliloquy is a stinging political satire about his private colony, the Congo Free State. Reports of outrageous exploitation and grotesque abuses led to widespread international protest in the early 1900s, arguably the first large-scale human rights movement. In the soliloquy, the King argues that bringing Christianity to the country outweighs a little starvation. Leopold's rubber gatherers were tortured, maimed and slaughtered until the movement forced Brussels to call a halt.

During the Philippine–American War, Twain wrote a short pacifist story titled The War Prayer, which makes the point that humanism and Christianity's preaching of love are incompatible with the conduct of war. It was submitted to Harper's Bazaar for publication, but on March 22, 1905, the magazine rejected the story as "not quite suited to a woman's magazine". Eight days later, Twain wrote to his friend Daniel Carter Beard, to whom he had read the story, "I don't think the prayer will be published in my time. None but the dead are permitted to tell the truth." Because he had an exclusive contract with Harper & Brothers, Twain could not publish The War Prayer elsewhere; it remained unpublished until 1923. It was republished as campaigning material by Vietnam War protesters.

Twain acknowledged that he had originally sympathized with the more moderate Girondins of the French Revolution and then shifted his sympathies to the more radical Sansculottes, indeed identifying himself as "a Marat" and writing that the Reign of Terror paled in comparison to the older terrors that preceded it. Twain supported the revolutionaries in Russia against the reformists, arguing that the Tsar must be got rid of by violent means, because peaceful ones would not work. He summed up his views of revolutions in the following statement:

> I am said to be a revolutionist in my sympathies, by birth, by breeding and by principle. I am always on the side of the revolutionists, because there never was a revolution unless there were some oppressive and intolerable conditions against which to revolute.

Civil rights

Twain was an adamant supporter of the abolition of slavery and the emancipation of slaves, even going so far as to say, "Lincoln's Proclamation ... not only set the black slaves free, but set the white man free also". He argued that non-whites did not receive justice in the United States, once saying, "I have seen Chinamen abused and maltreated in all the mean, cowardly ways possible to the invention of a degraded nature ... but I never saw a Chinaman righted in a court of justice for wrongs thus done to him". He paid for at least one black person to attend Yale Law School and for another black person to attend a southern university to become a minister.

Twain's sympathetic views on race were not reflected in his early writings on American Indians. Of them, Twain wrote in 1870:

> His heart is a cesspool of falsehood, of treachery, and of low and devilish instincts. With him, gratitude is an unknown emotion; and when one does him a kindness, it is safest to keep the face toward him, lest the reward be an arrow in the back. To accept of a favor from him is

to assume a debt which you can never repay to his satisfaction, though you bankrupt yourself trying. The scum of the earth!

As counterpoint, Twain's essay on "The Literary Offenses of Fenimore Cooper" offers a much kinder view of Indians. "No, other Indians would have noticed these things, but Cooper's Indians never notice anything. Cooper thinks they are marvelous creatures for noticing, but he was almost always in error about his Indians. There was seldom a sane one among them." In his later travelogue Following the Equator (1897), Twain observes that in colonized lands all over the world, "savages" have always been wronged by "whites" in the most merciless ways, such as "robbery, humiliation, and slow, slow murder, through poverty and the white man's whiskey"; his conclusion is that "there are many humorous things in this world; among them the white man's notion that he is less savage than the other savages". In an expression that captures his East Indian experiences, he wrote, "So far as I am able to judge nothing has been left undone, either by man or Nature, to make India the most extraordinary country that the sun visits on his rounds. Where every prospect pleases, and only man is vile."

Twain was also a staunch supporter of women's rights and an active campaigner for women's suffrage. His "Votes for Women" speech, in which he pressed for the granting of voting rights to women, is considered one of the most famous in history.

Helen Keller benefited from Twain's support as she pursued her college education and publishing despite her disabilities and financial limitations. The two were friends for roughly 16 years.

Through Twain's efforts, the Connecticut legislature voted a pension for Prudence Crandall, since 1995 Connecticut's official heroine, for her efforts towards the education of African-American young ladies in Connecticut. Twain also offered to purchase for her use her former house in Canterbury, home of the Canterbury Female Boarding School, but she declined.

Labor

Twain wrote glowingly about unions in the river boating industry in

94

Life on the Mississippi, which was read in union halls decades later. He supported the labor movement, especially one of the most important unions, the Knights of Labor. In a speech to them, he said:

> Who are the oppressors? The few: the King, the capitalist, and a handful of other overseers and superintendents. Who are the oppressed? The many: the nations of the earth; the valuable personages; the workers; they that make the bread that the soft-handed and idle eat.

Religion

Twain was a Presbyterian. He was critical of organized religion and certain elements of Christianity through his later life. He wrote, for example, "Faith is believing what you know ain't so", and "If Christ were here now there is one thing he would not be – a Christian". With anti-Catholic sentiment rampant in 19th century America, Twain noted he was "educated to enmity toward everything that is Catholic". As an adult, he engaged in religious discussions and attended services, his theology developing as he wrestled with the deaths of loved ones and with his own mortality.

Twain generally avoided publishing his most controversial opinions on religion in his lifetime, and they are known from essays and stories that were published later. In the essay Three Statements of the Eighties in the 1880s, Twain stated that he believed in an almighty God, but not in any messages, revelations, holy scriptures such as the Bible, Providence, or retribution in the afterlife. He did state that "the goodness, the justice, and the mercy of God are manifested in His works", but also that "the universe is governed by strict and immutable laws", which determine "small matters", such as who dies in a pestilence. At other times, he wrote or spoke in ways that contradicted a strict deist view, for example, plainly professing a belief in Providence. In some later writings in the 1890s, he was less optimistic about the goodness of God, observing that "if our Maker is all-powerful for good or evil, He is not in His right mind". At other times, he conjectured sardonically that perhaps God had created the world with all its tortures for some purpose of His own, but was otherwise indifferent to humanity, which was too petty and insignificant to deserve His attention anyway.

In 1901, Twain criticized the actions of the missionary Dr. William Scott Ament (1851–1909) because Ament and other missionaries had collected indemnities from Chinese subjects in the aftermath of the Boxer Uprising of 1900. Twain's response to hearing of Ament's methods was published in the North American Review in February 1901: To the Person Sitting in Darkness, and deals with examples of imperialism in China, South Africa, and with the U.S. occupation of the Philippines. A subsequent article, "To My Missionary Critics" published in The North American Review in April 1901, unapologetically continues his attack, but with the focus shifted from Ament to his missionary superiors, the American Board of Commissioners for Foreign Missions.

After his death, Twain's family suppressed some of his work that was especially irreverent toward conventional religion, including Letters from the Earth, which was not published until his daughter Clara reversed her position in 1962 in response to Soviet propaganda about the withholding. The anti-religious The Mysterious Stranger was published in 1916. Little Bessie, a story ridiculing Christianity, was first published in the 1972 collection Mark Twain's Fables of Man.

He raised money to build a Presbyterian Church in Nevada in 1864.

Twain created a reverent portrayal of Joan of Arc, a subject over which he had obsessed for forty years, studied for a dozen years and spent two years writing about. In 1900 and again in 1908 he stated, "I like Joan of Arc best of all my books, it is the best".

Those who knew Twain well late in life recount that he dwelt on the subject of the afterlife, his daughter Clara saying: "Sometimes he believed death ended everything, but most of the time he felt sure of a life beyond."

Twain's frankest views on religion appeared in his final work Autobiography of Mark Twain, the publication of which started in November 2010, 100 years after his death. In it, he said:

There is one notable thing about our Christianity: bad, bloody, merciless, money-grabbing, and predatory as it is – in our country particularly and in all other Christian countries in a somewhat modified degree – it is still a hundred times better than the Christianity of the Bible, with its prodigious crime – the invention of Hell. Measured by our Christianity of to-day, bad as it is, hypocritical as it is, empty and hollow as it is, neither the Deity nor his Son is a Christian, nor qualified for that moderately high place. Ours is a terrible religion. The fleets of the world could swim in spacious comfort in the innocent blood it has spilled.

Twain was a Freemason. He belonged to Polar Star Lodge No. 79 A.F.&A.M., based in St. Louis. He was initiated an Entered Apprentice on May 22, 1861, passed to the degree of Fellow Craft on June 12, and raised to the degree of Master Mason on July 10.

Twain visited Salt Lake City for two days and met there members of The Church of Jesus Christ of Latter-day Saints. They also gave him a Book of Mormon. He later wrote in Roughing It about that book:

> The book seems to be merely a prosy detail of imaginary history, with the Old Testament for a model; followed by a tedious plagiarism of the New Testament.

Vivisection

Twain was opposed to the vivisection practices of his day. His objection was not on a scientific basis but rather an ethical one. He specifically cited the pain caused to the animal as his basis of his opposition:

> I am not interested to know whether Vivisection produces results that are profitable to the human race or doesn't. ... The pains which it inflicts upon unconsenting animals is the basis of my enmity towards it, and it is to me sufficient justification of the enmity without looking further.

Pen names

Twain used different pen names before deciding on "Mark Twain". He signed humorous and imaginative sketches as "Josh" until 1863. Additionally, he used the pen name "Thomas Jefferson Snodgrass" for a series of humorous letters.

He maintained that his primary pen name came from his years working on Mississippi riverboats, where two fathoms, a depth indicating water safe for the passage of boat, was a measure on the sounding line. Twain is an archaic term for "two", as in "The veil of the temple was rent in twain." The riverboatman's cry was "mark twain" or, more fully, "by the mark twain", meaning "according to the mark [on the line], [the depth is] two [fathoms]", that is, "The water is 12 feet (3.7 m) deep and it is safe to pass."

Twain said that his famous pen name was not entirely his invention. In Life on the Mississippi, he wrote:

> Captain Isaiah Sellers was not of literary turn or capacity, but he used to jot down brief paragraphs of plain practical information about the river, and sign them "MARK TWAIN", and give them to the New Orleans Picayune. They related to the stage and condition of the river, and were accurate and valuable; ... At the time that the telegraph brought the news of his death, I was on the Pacific coast. I was a fresh new journalist, and needed a nom de guerre; so I confiscated the ancient mariner's discarded one, and have done my best to make it remain what it was in his hands – a sign and symbol and warrant that whatever is found in its company may be gambled on as being the petrified truth; how I have succeeded, it would not be modest in me to say.

Twain's story about his pen name has been questioned by some with the suggestion that "mark twain" refers to a running bar tab that Twain would regularly incur while drinking at John Piper's saloon in Virginia City, Nevada. Samuel Clemens himself responded to this suggestion by saying, "Mark Twain was the nom de plume of one Captain Isaiah Sellers, who used to write river news over it for the New Orleans Picayune. He died in 1869 and as he could no longer need that signature, I laid violent hands upon it without asking permission of the proprietor's remains. That is the history of the nom de plume I bear."

In his autobiography, Twain writes further of Captain Sellers' use of "Mark Twain":

> I was a cub pilot on the Mississippi River then, and one day

I wrote a rude and crude satire which was leveled at Captain Isaiah Sellers, the oldest steamboat pilot on the Mississippi River, and the most respected, esteemed, and revered. For many years he had occasionally written brief paragraphs concerning the river and the changes which it had undergone under his observation during fifty years, and had signed these paragraphs "Mark Twain" and published them in the St. Louis and New Orleans journals. In my satire I made rude game of his reminiscences. It was a shabby poor performance, but I didn't know it, and the pilots didn't know it. The pilots thought it was brilliant. They were jealous of Sellers, because when the gray-heads among them pleased their vanity by detailing in the hearing of the younger craftsmen marvels which they had seen in the long ago on the river, Sellers was always likely to step in at the psychological moment and snuff them out with wonders of his own which made their small marvels look pale and sick. However, I have told all about this in "Old Times on the Mississippi." The pilots handed my extravagant satire to a river reporter, and it was published in the New Orleans True Delta. That poor old Captain Sellers was deeply wounded. He had never been held up to ridicule before; he was sensitive, and he never got over the hurt which I had wantonly and stupidly inflicted upon his dignity. I was proud of my performance for a while, and considered it quite wonderful, but I have changed my opinion of it long ago. Sellers never published another paragraph nor ever used his nom de guerre again.

Legacy and depictions

Trademark white suit

While Twain is often depicted wearing a white suit, modern representations suggesting that he wore them throughout his life are unfounded. Evidence suggests that Twain began wearing white suits on the lecture circuit, after the death of his wife Olivia ("Livy") in 1904. However, there is also evidence showing him wearing a white suit before 1904. In 1882, he sent a photograph of himself in a white suit to 18-year-old Edward W. Bok, later publisher of the Ladies Home Journal, with a handwritten dated note. The white suit did eventually become his trademark, as illustrated in

99

anecdotes about this eccentricity (such as the time he wore a white summer suit to a Congressional hearing during the winter). McMasters' The Mark Twain Encyclopedia states that Twain did not wear a white suit in his last three years, except at one banquet speech.

In his autobiography, Twain writes of his early experiments with wearing white out-of-season:

> Next after fine colors, I like plain white. One of my sorrows, when the summer ends, is that I must put off my cheery and comfortable white clothes and enter for the winter into the depressing captivity of the shapeless and degrading black ones. It is mid-October now, and the weather is growing cold up here in the New Hampshire hills, but it will not succeed in freezing me out of these white garments, for here the neighbors are few, and it is only of crowds that I am afraid. (Source wikipedia)

NOTABLE WORKS

NOVELS

The Gilded Age: A Tale of Today (1873)

The Prince and the Pauper (1881)

A Connecticut Yankee in King Arthur's Court (1889)

The American Claimant (1892)

Pudd'nhead Wilson (1894)

Personal Recollections of Joan of Arc (1896)

A Horse's Tale (1907)

The Mysterious Stranger (1916, posthumous)

TOM SAWYER AND HUCKLEBERRY FINN

The Adventures of Tom Sawyer (1876)

Adventures of Huckleberry Finn (1884)

Tom Sawyer Abroad (1894)

Tom Sawyer, Detective (1896)

"Schoolhouse Hill" (6 chapters) in The Mysterious Stranger (c.1898, unfinished)

"Huck Finn and Tom Sawyer among the Indians" (c. 1884, 9 chapters, unfinished)

"Huck Finn" (1903, unfinished)

"Tom Sawyer's Conspiracy" (10 chapters, unfinished)

"Tom Sawyer's Gang Plans a Naval Battle" (unfinished)

ADAM AND EVE

"Extracts from Adam's Diary", illustrated by Frederick Strothmann (1904)

"Eve's Diary", illustrated by Lester Ralph (1906)

"The Private Life of Adam and Eve: Being Extracts from Their Diaries, Translated from the Original Mss." – posthumous issue of the 1904 and 1906 works bound as one, as Twain had requested in a recently discovered letter

SHORT STORIES

"The Celebrated Jumping Frog of Calaveras County" (1865)

"Advice to Little Girls" (1865)

"General Washington's Negro Body-Servant" (1868)

"Cannibalism in the Cars" (1868)

"My Late Senatorial Secretaryship" (1868)

"A Ghost Story" (1870)

"A True Story, Repeated Word for Word As I Heard It" (1874)

"Some Learned Fables for Good Old Boys and Girls" (1875)

"The Story Of The Bad Little Boy" (1875)

"The Story Of The Good Little Boy" (1875)

"A Literary Nightmare" (1876)

"A Murder, a Mystery, and a Marriage" (1876)

"The Canvasser's Tale" (1876)

"The Invalid's Story" (1877)

"The Great Revolution in Pitcairn" (1879)

"1601: Conversation, as it was by the Social Fireside, in the Time of the Tudors" (1880)

"The McWilliamses and the Burglar Alarm" (1882)

"The Stolen White Elephant" (1882)

"Luck" (1891)

"Those Extraordinary Twins" (1892)

"The Esquimau Maiden's Romance" (1893)

"The Million Pound Bank Note" (1893)

"The Man That Corrupted Hadleyburg" (1900)

"A Double Barrelled Detective Story" (1902)

"A Dog's Tale" (1904)

"The War Prayer" (1905)

"Hunting the Deceitful Turkey" (1906)

"A Fable" (1909)

"Captain Stormfield's Visit to Heaven" (1909)

"My Platonic Sweetheart" (1912, posthumous)

"The Purloining of Prince Oleomargarine" (2017, posthumous)

COLLECTIONS

SHORT STORY COLLECTIONS

The Celebrated Jumping Frog of Calaveras County and Other Sketches (1867), short story collection

Mark Twain's (Burlesque) Autobiography and First Romance (1871), short story collection

Sketches New and Old (1875), short story collection

A True Story and the Recent Carnival of Crime (1877), short story collection

Punch, Brothers, Punch! and Other Sketches (1878), short story collection

Mark Twain's Library of Humor (1888), short story collection

Merry Tales (1892), short story collection

The £1,000,000 Bank Note and Other New Stories (1893), short story collection

The $30,000 Bequest and Other Stories (1906), short story collection

The Curious Republic of Gondour and Other Whimsical Sketches (1919, posthumous), short story collection

The Washoe Giant in San Francisco (1938, posthumous), short story collection

Mark Twain's Fables of Man (1972, posthumous), short story collection

ESSAY COLLECTIONS

Memoranda (1870-1871), essay collection from Galaxy

How to Tell a Story and other Essays (1897)

Europe and Elsewhere (1923, posthumous), edited by Albert Bigelow Paine

Letters from the Earth (1962, posthumous)

A Pen Warmed Up In Hell (1972, posthumous)

The Bible According to Mark Twain (1996, posthumous)

ESSAYS

"On the Decay of the Art of Lying" (1880)

"The Awful German Language" (1880)

"Advice to Youth" (1882)

"Fenimore Cooper's Literary Offenses" (1895)

"English As She Is Taught" (1887)

"Concerning the Jews" (1898)

"A Salutation Speech From the Nineteenth Century to the Twentieth" (1900)

"To the Person Sitting in Darkness" (1901)

"To My Missionary Critics" (1901)

"Edmund Burke on Croker and Tammany" (1901)

"What Is Man?" (1906)

"Christian Science" (1907)

"Queen Victoria's Jubilee" (1910)

"The United States of Lyncherdom" (1923, posthumous)

NON-FICTION

The Innocents Abroad (1869), travel

Roughing It (1872), travel

Old Times on the Mississippi (1876), travel

A Tramp Abroad (1880), travel

Life on the Mississippi (1883), travel

Following the Equator (sometimes titled "More Tramps Abroad") (1897), travel

Is Shakespeare Dead? (1909)

Moments with Mark Twain (1920, posthumous)

Mark Twain's Notebook (1935, posthumous)

Letters from Hawaii (letters written in 1866, published as a book in 1947)

OTHER WRITINGS

Is He Dead? (1898), play

"The Battle Hymn of the Republic, Updated" (1901), satirical lyric

King Leopold's Soliloquy (1905), satire

"Little Bessie Would Assist Providence" (1908), poem

Slovenly Peter (1935, posthumous), children's book

"Some Thoughts on the Science of Onanism" (1879), a speech given to The Stomach Club.

AUTOBIOGRAPHY AND LETTERS

Mark Twain's Autobiography

> Chapters from My Autobiography published by North American Review (1906–1907)
>
> Posthumous edition compiled and edited by Albert Bigelow Paine (1924)
>
> Posthumous edition named Mark Twain in Eruption compiled and edited by Bernard DeVoto (1940)
>
> Posthumous edition compiled and edited by Charles Neider
>
> Posthumous edition compiled and edited by Harriet Elinor Smith and the Mark Twain Project: Volume 1 (2010)
>
> Posthumous edition compiled and edited by Robert Hirst and the Mark Twain Project: Volume 2 (2013)
>
> Posthumous edition compiled and edited by Harriet Elinor Smith and the Mark Twain Project: Volume 3 (2015)

Mark Twain's Letters, 1853–1880 (2010, posthumous)

"Territorial Enterprise letters" being compiled for release in 2017

CPSIA information can be obtained
at www.ICGtesting.com
Printed in the USA
LVHW031954210720
661242LV00019B/998